TRUE COLORS OF FILMIC FAIRIES

KHURSHID ALAM

TRUE COLORS OF FILMIC FAIRIES

Author: Khurshid Alam
Translated from the Urdu book "Filmi Pariyo Key Par Purzey" by Khurshid Alam.

Original Publishers: Primetime Publications

Translator: Waqas Hafeez
Editors: Saad Khan, Harris Gondal
Cover Design: Saqib Arshad

Printed in the United States of America

Dedicated to Mr. Muhammad Yasin Goreja who spent fifty years of his life in the service of film industry and film journalism.

KHURSHID ALAM

A heartfelt gratitude to Omar Ali Khan for
donating his personally signed copy of the
book "Filmi Pariyo Key Par Purzey" to
Khajistan Press.

To a life spent in longing
and spent in drawing your pictures

AMJAD ISLAM AMJAD

CONTENTS

PREFACE

This book is my second attempt. Before this, I had written a book on the personality of Khawaja Ghulam Farid named "Tradition of Study on Fareed in Pakistan." That book was very popular in South Punjab.

You must be wondering why I suddenly wrote a book on movies after writing about the Saraiki poet, Khawaja Ghulam Fareed. The answer is that whenever I would read any newspaper, periodicals or film magazines for information regarding the film industry, many questions would be left unanswered. So, one day I thought why not write a book that has as much information as possible about film actresses, and their personal lives as well as film careers.

I faced many issues while writing this book, but the kind people listed below helped me a lot in solving those issues.

- M. Yusuf: I am grateful to M. Yusuf, Chief Editor – Shama Lahore, who co-operated with me despite his illness.

- Tufail Akhtar: Tufail Akhtar is a well-known personality. His way of talking is so interesting that one does not want to leave his company. He has been serving the industry as a film journalist for the past forty years. I am grateful to him that he supported me in making the material available despite his immensely busy schedule.

- Mr. Yasin Goreja: He holds a prominent position in film literature. His services are invaluable for the film industry. I only had the imagination of the book in my mind but Mr. Goreja gave this imagination a reality. His simple nature impressed me a lot and that is why I have dedicated my book to him.

The book is divided into nine chapters which include mentions of Babra Sharif, Sangeeta & Kavita, Mussrat Shaheen, Nadira, Neeli, Mumtaz, Anjuman, Reema and Saima. Please read this book and give your feedback.

Thanks,
Khurshid Alam
Kot Abdul Hakeem (Khanewal District)

COUNTING THE WINGS OF A FLYING BIRD & CLIPPING THE WINGS OF A MOVING FAIRY

Counting the wings of a flying bird is one thing and counting the wings of a flying fairy is another. Like seeing faces is one thing and reading them is another, and writing their story is yet a completely different thing. That work is either done by a millionaire or by one of the millions. This is the reason why hundreds of pages of magazines and journals are filled with the glamor of stars, the flight and landing of fairies, but there is not a single word of importance or record in them. This is because there is not a person among those writers who is in the know of inner secrets, as of yet. Those who could dare did not write anything and those who were expected to do so remained silent because of expediency. So how could one know about the inner secrets? All we have is the dust of hearsay and the fog of rumors, which have made the faces dimmer and the impressions blurred. Therefore, we are forced to be content with whatever is available and consider the raw writing to be history. So, whatever is popular out there is all nonsense.

In his youth, Khursheed Alam once came to Lahore from afar and brought the far-fetched question: why is our film information so scant? Despite the fact that a large number of people want to read the stories of filmic jinn and fairies, and they occupy their day's thoughts and night's dreams. Muhammad Yasin Goreja and I told him back-to-back that he should start the project because we both knew that his observation was weak but his study was very powerful. He is an educated and knowledgeable person. Coming to Pak Studies, he has written the play "Modern Children" and a "Study on Ghulam Fareed." Since our suggestion was not merely entertaining, it touched his heart and he started to write and compile "True Colors of Filmic Fairies," and the next time when he came from Abdul-Hakim to Lahore, he had cut the wings of many famous fairies.

Khurshid Alam's ancestors come from the Ferozepur district. He himself was born in Abdul Hakim. His ancestors' profession is farming. He was employed in a gas company after completing his matriculation from Government High School; he has a BA from Government College Multan and an MA from Zakaria University. He is the husband of a wife and father of a son. He respects his mother and has compassion for his siblings as he is the eldest among them. He likes reading the newspaper and watching TV, hates lies and liars and loves truth and honest persons. He is a seeker of peace, love and a customer of civility and dignified conduct. Of course, that is why he has been compelled to set the pen in motion to compile an accurate history of people's favorite actresses and to guide future actresses.

The articles of Khurshid Alam are so simple that they can be accused of being blunt, and the way he talks is so innocent that we feel an uncontrollable love for him like we often feel for children. Nevertheless, the good news is that those who want to know about film stars and those who want to read film material may find in him a straightforward writer from whom much better work can be expected going forward. Most things become attractive with beautification, but simplicity has a beauty in itself, the buyers of which are not diminishing in number, even today. This first Pakistani showbiz book of Khurshid Alam is very important for these simple people.

Tufail Akhtar
Editor, Monthly "Muskurahat" Lahore.

Babra Sahrif

BABRA SHARIF

From Jet Washing Powder to "Samaaj"

Family Background

The red-light district continues to provide priceless diamonds for the film industry. Many famous actresses and musicians came to the film industry from this area and have raised flags of success.

Many years ago, there lived a man named Sharif in the red-light district of Lahore who was very poor. He had a hard life and used to sell ghee in front of the Globe Hotel in the red-light district. People used to call him Sharif Gheewala. His house was located a few steps away from the Globe Hotel. People usually refer to the houses located in the red-light district as "brothels." Nowadays these houses (brothels) have been rented out to respectable people.

Sharif's income was very low, so it was very difficult to survive. He often thought that someday his good time would come and he too would be able to live a prosperous life.

Sharif had three daughters and a son. The daughters' names were Firdous, Fakhira and Babra, while the son's name was Talat.

Months and years passed and Sharif's daughters became young women. Sharif was increasingly hopeful that his days of poverty would end. When Firdous became a young woman, she started modeling in addition to singing, which started to increase Sharif's income. One day, Sharif received a huge amount of money from a Seth to deflower Firdous. Now he had a decent amount of money. In second place was Fakhira, and she too was influenced by seeing her sister. There were often singing parties in Sharif's house. One day a Seth fell in love with Fakhira. Fakhira also gave a very positive response and both of them expressed love through their eyes. After a few days, Fakhira left the brothel and fled with the Seth. Sharif was not at all panicked by Fakhira's eloping as he was sure that his daughter would surely return, as prostitutes never actually leave their brothels. After a few days, Fakhira returned to her home after impoverishing the Seth and looting all his wealth.

At that time, Babra was younger but not innocent. She was watching the conduct of her two elder sisters, learning their tricks. She also started singing at home and modeling as well. Babra appeared in an advertisement for jet washing powder on Pakistan Television, which made her famous.

Due to the popularity of the ad, Pakistan Television offered Babra Sharif a role in a drama called "Kiran Kahani." When Babra acted in that drama, her role became the talk of the town in Pakistan. The Seth whom Fakhira had impoverished belonged to the Memon community. When his community saw the condition of their Memon brother, they decided to take revenge on Sharif and his daughter. Sharif came to know about their plan in time and returned to Lahore with his family.

When he came to Lahore, he first bought the Globe Hotel. And then he started living in his house fearlessly. The people of the red-light district became envious after seeing his financial condition and some became jealous of him. Some people contemptuously started calling him Sharif Gheewala to remind him of his former position, but Sharif did not care about anyone. But he faced trouble when Firdous fell in love with a singer and squandered his wealth on the man. Firdous also built a bungalow for him in Gujarat, left the house and fled with the singer.

The singer took away all the wealth from Firdous and threw her out of the house. By that time, Firdaus had become a mother of two children. The two children are still with Firdaus and have grown up.

Although Sharif had now acquired a lot of wealth, his lust for more was increasing. So, he started visiting the studios to make his daughters film heroines. First, he took Fakhira to Shabab Kiranvi.

Shabab Kiranvi kept Fakhira with him for some time, giving her the chance in his film "Insaf Aur Qanoon." The film was released on April 16, 1971. It was an average film in terms of business. As smart as Fakhira Sharif was in ordinary life, she could not succeed in films. She got roles in only a few films but did not get any special response from the public. Finally, Aslam Dar's film "Pehli Nazar," released on 16 October, 1977, turned out to be her last film.

Deflowering of Babra Sharif

In the red-light district, the ritual of deflowering is performed with great fervor. Deflowering is like a wedding night for a new bride. A wedding night comes only once in a normal girl's life, but in deflowering, a person is charged a lot of money for the first time, and after that, anyone who comes can sleep with that girl by paying the required amount.

After the drama "Kiran Kahani," director S. Sulaiman signed Babra Sharif for his film "Intezar" in 1974. In those days, a well-known personality stayed at the Hotel Intercontinental. He called Babra there and signed the contract. The next morning, when Babra returned home, Sharif was very happy because his daughter had brought her one night's income home in a sack and it was much more than Sharif's expectations. So Babra was deflowered in this way.

When Sharif became rich enough, he left the red-light district because it was no longer in his honor to live there. Like other famous actors, he came to Gulberg with his family.

Babra Sharif's Appearance in Films

When Fakhira used to come to the set of "Insan Aur Aadmi" at Shah Noor Studio, she used to be accompanied by a young girl. The color of that girl was fair and her face was rosy. She looked ten years old, but her physical features suggested that she was a virgin of nineteen to twenty years. She used to sit quietly on one side of the set and watch her sister work with great interest. She never did any mischief to disturb the atmosphere of the set. Everyone would look at her because she was so attractive. That girl was Babra Sharif.

Fakhira and Firdous were busy trying to introduce her in the film industry. For this they had also spoken to Shamim Aara. Filmmaker Shamim Aara and director S. Sulaiman selected her for a side role in the film "Bhool." The other cast of that film included Munawar Zarif, Mumtaz, Shabnam and Nadeem. Munawar Zarif guided Babra Sharif a lot in that film. The film was released on November 1, 1974 and became a success.

After that, Babra started getting work in films. After Shabnam, Babra is the only actress to work in Urdu films for such a long time. Whether a film succeeded or failed, Babra would be at the pinnacle of the art. Be it tragedy, comedy, romance, the role of a playful girl or the role of a blind girl, Babra would fill the role with the color of reality.

List of Famous Films of Babra Sharif

Film's Name	Language	Director	Outcome	Release Year
Intezar	Urdu	S. Suleman	Successful	9-Aug-1974
Bhool	Urdu	S. Suleman	Successful	1-Nov-1974
Shama	Urdu	Nazar Shabab	Successful	25-Dec-1974
Mera naam paaty Khan	Punjabi	Masood Pervaiz	Unsuccessful	21-Mar-1975
Mera Naam hai Mohabbat	Urdu	Shabab Keranvi	Successful	8-Aug-1975
Talaash	Urdu	Pervaiz Malik	Successful	23-Jan-1976
Anjaam	Punjabi	Waheed Dar	Average	30-Apr-1976
Dekha jai ga	Urdu	Jan Muhamad	Successful	18-Jun-1976
Sulakhein	Urdu	Hassan Askari	Successful	23-Dec-1977
Prince	Urdu	S. Suleman	Successful	30-Jun-1978
Playboy	Urdu	Shamim Aara	Successful	5-Sep-1978
Yeh Zamana Aur hai	Urdu	Shabab Keranvi	Successful	9-Oct-1981
Sangdill	Urdu	Hassan Tariq	Successful	9-Oct-1981
Miss Columbo	Urdu	Shamim Aara	Successful	30-Jun-1984

Miss Singapore	Urdu	Shamim Aara	Successful	20-Jun-1985
Ajab Khan	Punjabi	Waheed Dar	Successful	2-Aug-1985
Haq Mehr	Punjabi	Iftekhar Khan	Average	8-Nov-1985
Miss Bangkok	Urdu	Iqbal Akhtar	Successful	17-Aug-1986
Mukhra	Punjabi	Iqbal Kashmiri	Successful	25-Jul-1988
Barish	Urdu	Altaf Hussain	Successful	29-Sep-1989
Gori Diyan Jhanjran	Punjabi	Usman Pirzada	Successful	19-Jan-1990
Zabata	Punjabi	Jahangir Mughal	Unsuccessful	3-Sep-1993
Sar-Kata Insaan	Punjabi	Average	Saeed Rizvi	22-Apr-1994

Babra Sharif acted in about 125 films in Urdu, Punjabi and Pashto. Babra Sharif worked with almost every director of her era but has not done a single film with a few directors of today including Syed Noor, Ajab Gul, Shaan, and Shahzad Rafique, etc.

"Mera Naam Hai Mohabbat" was the most successful film starring Babra Sharif and Ghulam Mohi-ud-Din. How that film was produced, the details are as follows: the director Shabab Keranvi went to London on a private visit. An English movie "Love Story" was being screened there, which was much talked about. He saw the movie in the cinema and was very impressed by it. The movie was made with a new hero and heroine. After returning from London, he started working on the movie. That time Nadeem and Shabnam were at their peak in the Pakistan film industry but they did not have time available. Shabab Keranvi gave a chance to new hero Ghulam Mohi-ud-Din with Babra Sharif. Ghulam Mohi-ud-Din was very happy with the decision of Shabab Keranvi because he got his first chance as a hero in the film. The film was released on August 8, 1975 after its completion and was a huge success. It won many awards and also did a lot of business in neighboring country China.

Babra Sharif's film "Barish" was completed in just 29 days. As it happened, "Barish" was being made by filmmaker Ghafoor Butt and director Haider Chaudhary. When it came to the cast of the film, director Haider Chaudhary proposed Kavita as the heroine, but filmmaker Ghafoor Butt liked Babra Sharif. When Ghafoor Butt did not listen to Haider Choudhary, he left Ghafoor Butt's film, cast Kavita and started making a film called "Barish." Meanwhile, Ghafoor Butt started making a film of the same name with director Altaf Hussain casting Babra Sharif as the heroine.

There was a lot of fighting between the two parties regarding the name of "Barish" and the matter reached the courts. Since both persons were making two films of the same name at the same time, the court took a very wise decision. It named Ghafoor Butt's film as "Barish" and Haider Chaudhary's film as "Paani."

After this fight, both of them started trying to complete the film in a hurry, in which Ghafoor Butt and director Altaf Hussain succeeded. They completed the film in 29 days and released it on September 29, 1989. Haider Choudhary's film got delayed for a few days because on those days Kavita's father Tayyab Rizvi was seriously ill in London and Kavita went to London due to this issue. Kavita completed the film on her return from London and thus "Paani" was released on 6 October, 1989. Both the films did good business. On his return from London, Tayyab Rizvi watched the movie "Paani" with his daughter, and he was really ashamed because she had filmed some nude scenes in the movie.

Love Affairs of Babra Sharif

Babra Sharif beat many heroines of the film industry in the matter of love. Love was a trivial thing for Babra Sharif. She had a long line of lovers whose details you will read below.

Babra Sharif and Ilyas Kashmiri

Ilyas Kashmiri is a very senior actor of the Pakistan film industry. He used to work in films even before the freedom of Pakistan. His debut film in Pakistan "Mundri" was released on August 28, 1949. The director of the film was Dawood Chand, Ilyas Kashmiri played the role of hero and Ragini was the heroine. Ilyas was a very handsome young man with a fair complexion and tall stature in his youth. He was very fond of beautiful girls and considered it his duty to welcome every girl who was joining the film industry.

During the days when Babra Sharif was trying to enter the film industry, Ilyas Kashmiri came forward, mentored her and arranged work for her in the films. In return, Ilyas Kashmiri spent several nights with Babra.

Babra Sharif and Munawar Zarif

Munawar Zarif was such a comedy artist in the Pakistani film industry that when he came onto the screen, people would start laughing even before he spoke. Even today, many comedians are copying Munawar Zarif. Munawar Zarif started with small roles in films and became the hero of films within a few years.

When Babra Sharif joined the film industry, at that time Munawar Zarif was ruling the industry as a successful hero.

Babra Sharif had collected all the history of Munawar Zarif, so she decided to approach him. On November 1, 1974, Babra Sharif and Munawar Zarif appeared together on the screen in the movie "Bhool."

Munawar Zarif was a lively person and fell in love with Babra Sharif out of mischief. The film world did not know about the affair because Babra Sharif was very smart and did not let anything out. On the other hand, Munawar Zarif was also cautious as he was a married man.

In the beginning, Babra Sharif also responded to Munawar Zarif's love with affection, but as Babra started getting more films, she grew apart from him. When Babra became a successful actress, at that time Munawar Zarif's position became completely worthless for Babra, so she gradually started avoiding Munawar Zarif.

On the other hand, Munawar started falling madly in love with Babra. The fire of love was burning his body but at that time Babra turned in another direction. Seeing all this, Munawar Zarif started drinking alcohol excessively, which caused him heart trouble. His friends suggested him to stop drinking but he did not listen to anyone. The heartache had taken a new direction. On the advice of friends, he went to America for a medical examination. The American doctors gave him a thorough check-up and told him that he would not live for more than a few months. The doctors' predictions came true and he died a few months later on April 29, 1976. Not even a single tear fell from Babra Sharif's eyes. She only spoke a few words of sympathy to show the people. Babra Sharif is responsible for the death of a lovely artist like Munawar Zarif but she does not realize it.

Babra Sharif's Love with Arab States

Babra Sharif was very fond of the Arab states. She used to go there and collect large sums of money from Arab sheikhs. Whenever she needed a lot of money, she would visit the Arab states. The path of the Arab states was shown to Babra Sharif by a man named Ijaz, alias Jaji. It so happened that one of Babra's friends was the actress Chhum who used to do small roles in the films. Her brother Jaji used to supply girls to Arab sheikhs. Once he presented a girl named Baby Rifat and Babra to an Arab. The Arab liked Babra and the poor Baby Rifat was left speechless. That was Babra's first visit, which was very successful. After that, Babra made it her routine.

Regarding the visits to the aforementioned Arab states, the weekly "Ujala" recorded on page 13 of its publication of July 15, 1977 that:

> "It is said that ever since Babra finished her tour of the Arab states, her stomach is constantly aching. If the pain is temporary, even the most cowardly person can bear it, but if the pain becomes permanent, then the bravest will lose their patience. Poor Babra is a young and delicate girl, so this constant pain would be very disturbing for her. We think, lest there be loss instead of gaining something. If there is a permanent defect in the human body, sometimes it does not go away even after spending millions of rupees. Poor Babra has to do a lot of work now."

After the above article in the weekly "Ujala," people all over the country made a lot of talk including some obscene jokes which are not possible to record here.

Babra Sharif and Shahid

When Babra Sharif turned away from Munawar Zarif, she saw various heroes around her to find some relief for her thirsty soul. Ghulam Muhyiddin's looks and appearance were ordinary, while Waheed Murad and Muhammad Ali were somewhat overaged. So, she was attracted to the actor Nadeem. First of all, he was married and secondly, he was very interested in the actress Mumtaz in those days, so Babra's love remained one-sided and unrequited.

Shahid was the only hero who lived up to her standards. The successful meeting of Shahid and Babra Sharif took place in the film "Dekha Jai Ga," directed by John Muhammad Juman, which was released on 18 June, 1976.

Shahid's Past

Shahid had been appearing in films since 1971. He was a married man with a homely wife named Dr. Munazza. Apart from that, Shahid was also introduced to films by a woman named "Seema." Seema Begum used to play character roles in films and often played the role of a mother. She played the role of Sultan Rahi's sister-in-law in the famous film Maula Jutt. She loved Shahid a lot. Since the prostitute (Seema) had loved Shahid herself, Shahid's fortune flourished. Apart from Seema, the actress Zamurd was also Shahid's wife and he also had a daughter called Urooj with her.

Babra's Marriage

Babra Sharif knew about all the women in Shahid's past, including Dr. Munazza, Seema and Zamurd. But still she was getting closer to Shahid. The reason was that everyone called Shahid a womanizer. Whenever he was near a girl, he used to lament his deprivations. Shahid was deprived of his mother's love in his childhood, so he became mentally and psychologically ill. Babra's point of view was that she could cure Shahid. Babra's siblings and father strongly advised her not to go near Shahid but she took Shahid on as a challenge.

Babra's sympathy gradually turned into love and Shahid also started coming to Babra's house stealthily. Initially, Shahid used to sit in the drawing room and then return, but later he reached Babra's bedroom. Babra Sharif didn't even realize that Shahid had become so close to her that the distance between their bodies disappeared. Actually, the thing was that Shahid had a special kind of magnetic force. It was such an attraction that girls forgot to control themselves.

Finally, one day Babra decided to marry Shahid. Babra's family was very saddened by the decision as their golden bird was now going to fly elsewhere. The marriage of Shahid and Babra was arranged in Karachi, in the presence of a few close friends. On the same day, they left for London for their honeymoon, while filmmakers kept waiting for them in Lahore for their unfinished films.

One day they both suddenly returned to Lahore and the filmmakers regained their hopes. Babra had made an agreement with Shahid at the time of marriage that he would divorce Zamurd and also leave his daughter Urooj with Zamurd. On returning from London, Shahid divorced Zamurd.

Zamurd's Revenge

Upon receiving the divorce, Zamurd abused Shahid and Babra a lot. On the same day, she decided to take revenge upon Shahid. She put a tinkling anklet on the feet of Shahid's daughter and started teaching her mujra. Urooj had not got a special place in the movies, so Zamurd got her engaged in mujra. In the last few days of her dwindling marriage, there was a big mujra in Faisalabad in which Urooj stole the hearts of people. They were throwing notes at Zamurd and she was collecting them.

Babra's Return to Lahore

On returning to Lahore, Babra's friends heard the stories of the honeymoon in London from Babra. She said that Shahid was the best companion of solitude, and his presence gave her so much fun that one did not remain conscious of anything. These were the things that led to Babra's downfall. Babra's friends followed Shahid, they thought that they should also enjoy Shahid's solitude. As the girls were getting closer to Shahid, Babra was getting further away. The situation became that Shahid started coming late form his film shootings. Sometimes he would go to Islamabad and sometimes he would be on a tour to Karachi. He was a whimsical person, unable to stay in one place. Babra caught Shahid red-handed on several occasions but still there was no change in Shahid's behavior.

Babra's challenge that she would make Shahid a normal person remained only a challenge and could not be implemented.

Babra was very saddened by this incident; she thought that Shahid did the same to her as she did to Munawar Zarif. But still Babra did not lose heart and she found another person with whom to take revenge upon Shahid.

Shehzad Gul and Babra Sharif

When Babra looked around, her eyes stopped at one place. He was a handsome fair-skinned boy named Shahzad Gul who was waiting for Babra's temerities. He was the son of Agha G.A. Gul, owner of Ever-new Studios. As Babra's films were often shot at Ever-new Studios, there was no difficulty in dating Shahzad Gul.

Babra was slowly getting closer to him. His family told her that they were respectable people, they had a high position in society, so it would be good if she stayed away from their son. But Babra did not agree because she only wanted to make Shahid jealous. The situation of their dating became such that Shahzad Gul's office had become Babra Sharif's make-up room. Being with Babra was Shahzad Gul's first love because he was a very shy young man. Babra did not have to work hard to trap him because she was a very smart woman. People from as far as the United Arab Emirates were caught in the trap of her coquetries.

Shahzad Gul and Babra were swinging in the cradle of love and enjoying the beautiful seasons of life. On the other hand, Shahid was very hurt by Babra's act. He thought: "Babra has insulted me, I left Zamurd for her, incurred the displeasure of my first wife Munazza, but Babra forgot my favors by befriending Shahzad Gul."

Finally, one night he made a decision and reached his in-laws. He openly admitted his mistake and asked his father-in-law to let Munazza come back home to him. Munazza also immediately forgave Shahid. He spent the night with his in-laws and came home the next morning with his wife Munazza. After the reconciliation, Shahid organized a grand dinner at the Hilton Hotel in Lahore, which was attended by his friends and loved ones. At the same time, he divorced Babra Sharif.

On the other hand, the incident of reconciliation was very sad for Babra Sharif. Along with this incident, a second incident was no less a blow for Babra. She suddenly got news that Shahzad Gul's marriage had been finalized with a domestic girl in Peshawar. The wedding date had been fixed and the friends had received the wedding cards. For Babra, that moment was no less than the doomsday and she was not able to comprehend anything.

On the one hand, the reconciliation of Shahid and Munazza.
On the other hand, Shahid's divorce to Babra.
On the third side, Shahzad Gul's wedding cards.

All the above scenes were playing in Babra's mind as if a sad movie was on. In that troubled state, Babra called Shehzad Gul, but he did not give a reasonable answer to Babra.

Babra was very upset with the whole situation. She regained consciousness with great difficulty. At that time, she had lost everything. By making Shahid jealous, she herself burnt. She suffered from depression and became so irritable that she would get angry at the slightest unpleasantness. She stopped communicating with anyone. She used to remember beautiful days lying in a closed room and would cry for hours. "What kind of revenge fate has taken on me. I wish, I had not rejected the love of a lively person like Munawar Zarif. Today I have lost everything. I wish I had not done that."

Shahid Surrounded by Charmers

It was only a few days after Munazza came back that another charmer of the film industry named Ishrat Chaudhary fell for Shahid. She often used to do club dancing, etc. in movies and was referred to by the name of Sex Kitten.

Ishrat Chaudhary also belonged to the red-light district. She thought that no one from the red-light district could take control of Shahid as she would get him tied with her. Ishrat Chaudhary married Shahid and moved to Canada for a few years. But as you know, Shahid was known as a womanizer and he could not stay in one place for long, so he could not stay with Ishrat for a longer period either.

The actress Mumtaz also tried hard to take control of Shahid. Shahid wanted to marry Mumtaz, but the actress Bahaar informed Mumtaz about Shahid's nature at the right time. Mumtaz had already experienced the hardship of marrying Ajmal Chaudhary, so she refused to marry Shahid.

Apart from Mumtaz, Sangeeta also extended the hand of friendship to Shahid, which I will describe in detail while writing the story of Sangeeta.

Fozia Ahmed (Arzoo)

Arzoo came to Lahore from Karachi around 1980–81.She also fell in love with Shahid. In 1981, director Jamshed Naqvi's film "I Love You" was being produced, during the filming of which the love between the two developed, but could not last for long. The movie "I Love You" was released on March 12, 1982. Just like the movie "I Love You" failed, so did their love.

A Few Famous Movies of Shahid

Film's Name	Language	Director	Release Year
Ansoo	Urdu	S.A. Bukhari	30-Jul-1971
Tehzib	Urdu	Hassan Tariq	20-Nov-1971
Aik Raat	Urdu	Jameel Akhtar	29-Sep-1972
Umrao Jaan Ada	Urdu	Hassan Tariq	29-Dec-1972
Pehla Waar	Punjabi	Diljeet Mirza	28-Oct-1973
Shikaar	Urdu	S.A. Hafiz	23-Aug-1974
Naukar Wohti Da	Punjabi	Haider Chaudhry	26-Jul-1974
Jadu	Punjabi	Iqbal Kashmiri	21-Feb-1975
Hewaan	Urdu	S.A. Hafiz	31-Dec-1975
Talaaq	Urdu	S. Suleman	14-May-1976
Dekha Jai Ga	Urdu	Jaan Muhammad	18-jun-1976
Surraya Bhopali	Urdu	S. Suleman	25-Feb-1975
Shabana	Urdu	Nazar Shabab	12-Nov-1976
Uff Yeh Biwiyan	Urdu	S. Suleman	25-Feb-1977
Begum Jaan	Urdu	Hassan Tariq	24-Jun-1977
Mirza Jutt	Punjabi	Masood Pervaiz	28-Sep-1982

Shahid and Firdous

Firdous played the role of Shahid's mother in S.A. Bukhari's film "Ansu." Shahid used to consider Firdous to be a mother even in his normal life, but Firdous had a different perspective for Shahid. The film completed but Firdous remained attached to Shahid. When Firdous got closer to Shahid, he became convinced that she too had fallen in love with him. Shahid thought, "Why not do another hunt?"

Firdous was senior to Shahid but in those days she had been rejected by Ijaz. She got Shahid addicted to various drugs. Before that, Shahid only drank alcohol. He began to feel more pleasure in these intoxicants. To get this pleasure, both of them would find a secluded place where no one would be near them. One night, he was caught intoxicated in the Mayani Sahib graveyard in Lahore. The next day, the morning papers published their night's activities.

Shahid's life is full of such incidents. Seeing that situation, filmmakers stopped casting Shahid in films. The reason was that they felt Shahid was not working in films seriously, he was only having affairs with some girl or other all the time. Similarly, one day a strange news story came to light which is recorded on page 213 of "Nigar Golden Jubilee" No. 2000. The news was that a lady named "Asma or Saima," who was caught drug smuggling at Istanbul Port, Turkey, and who had been sentenced to death by the court there, claimed to be the wife of Shahid with proof of it.

On one hand the filmmakers stopped casting Shahid and on the other hand Shahid was also not able to work mentally anymore, so he left the film industry. He grew a beard and started spending more time in worship. For a long time, he stayed at Data Darbar, Lahore to wash away his previous sins.

In February 2001, Sardar Ghaffar, a lover of the actress Firdous, was arrested on charges of corruption. Mr. Sardar built Firdous Market in Gulbarg for Firdous, which is still owned by her. It should be noted that Sardar Ghaffar is the brother of the former prime minister of Azad Kashmir, Sardar Abdul Qayyum Khan.

Babra Sharif and Faisal

After Shahzad Gul's marriage, Babra immediately turned to his brother Sajjad Gul. The net of love thrown by Babra towards Sajjad Gul could not ensnare him. He did not respond to her audacity, which made Babra very upset. But she did not give up. Her next victim was the new young hero Faisal. His full name is Faisal-ur-Rehman and he is the son of famous photographer, Masood-ur-Rehman. The famous actor Rehman was Faisal's uncle. His film career is not that long but he still has some excellent films to his credit.

Faisal's debut film "Nahi Abhi Nahi" was directed by Nazar-ul-Islam and released on 21 October 1980. He was less than 20 years old at the time. Babra Sharif and Faisal came together for the first time in director Iqbal Kashmiri's film "Aladdin," which was released on August 2, 1981.

Faisal was a handsome boy whom Babra had been searching for a long time. She needed a young man like Faisal to forget her old sorrows. She slowly started coming closer to Faisal who was not so mature but was physically young. He liked Babra's boldness.

Faisal and Babra became closer in a true sense when Shamim Aara went abroad with the unit of her film "Miss Colombo." Since Shamim Aara had to complete her film soon, she did not disturb Babra and Faisal's privacy much. However, she was aware of Babra and Shahid's affair and the trauma Babra was going through. Babra and Faisal took full advantage of the solitude abroad. They both came so close to each other that it was as if they had discovered each other. With the closeness of Faisal, Babra felt as if someone had given water to a dry tree, and the ache of her heart began to waver.

When the news of their love reached Pakistan, the filmmakers began casting the new couple increasingly. Shamim Aara cast them a second time in her film "Miss Singapore," reuniting them again. As this was Faisal's first love, he was inexperienced and emotional. As soon as Faisal got frank with Babra, she became more cautious because now she started fearing her infamy.

A couple of their films did not perform well at the box office, after which Babra started to distance herself from Faisal. Whenever Faisal wanted to talk and be close to her, she would turn her face to the other side, making Faisal very sad.

Faisal was deeply affected by Babra's heartlessness and he became addicted to drugs. Thus, he used to consume more and more drugs to forget his sorrow.

Film makers stopped casting Faisal after the failure of a few more of his films. He could not bear the shock and became very emaciated and weak. He was feeling as if Babra was taking revenge for her separation from Shahid. Faisal's condition worsened, his hair fell out and he became bald. Seeing his condition, Faisal left the industry on his own.

He managed to recover after many years, underwent a hair transplant and is currently working in television dramas. His beautiful drama "Bulandi" aired some time ago, which was produced by Kashif Mehmood who is also an actor.

Babra Sharif and Ayaz

Babra got temporary relief after cutting Faisal out of her life. But as the days passed by, she started feeling lonely. Since Faisal was no longer working with her, it was impossible to contact him. Faisal was a young guy and since Babra enjoyed the beautiful days of her life being close to a young person, she found another young man named Ayaz Naik. "Nahi Abhi Nahi" was the debut film of Ayaz too.

Babra was excited when she was cast alongside Ayaz in "Yeh Zamana Aur Hai," directed by Shabab Keranvi. It was released on 19 October 1981 and became a huge success. Ayaz and Babra became friends after the success of the film. After that,

Shabab Keranvi cast them both in his film "Aik Din Bahu Ka," which was released on 22 June 1982. The two got to know each other very well during the shooting of the film. As usual, Babra slowly started to develop a relationship with Ayaz. She was afraid that Ayaz would also leave her lonely. So, she gave Ayaz the chance to get closer to her and thus Ayaz reached Babra's bedroom. Because Ayaz was younger than Babra, he was boisterous, emotional and often behaved childishly. He even started telling other people about Babra and his relationship. The situation was very disturbing for Babra, and she tried hard to make him understand but all in vain. He wanted to prove his superiority everywhere but did not realize that Babra did not accept anyone's superiority. Babra realized that she had befriended a foolish person.

In those days, Hasan Askari's film "Aik Duje Ke Liye" was under production. Babra had decided that after the completion of the film, she would throw Ayaz out of her life. Finally, the film was completed and released on May 6, 1993 and Babra was relieved. After that, she strictly stopped Ayaz from coming near her.

Director Aslam Dar announced the making of a Punjabi film, "Ishq Nachave Gali," in which he offered Syed Noor the role of the hero but he refused, so then Aslam Dar cast Ayaz. Ayaz was cast opposite Durdana Rehman, who later became Aslam Dar's wife. The film was released on November 9, 1984 and was a huge success. It won six Nigar Awards.

Seeing the success of the film, director Nazar ul Islam cast Faisal along with Ayaz, but Babra Sharif did not allow them to come close to her and they both remained defeated. One of them was persecuted by Babra and to the other, Babra made starry eyes during the day. Despite being in a successful film like "Ishq Nachave Gali," Ayaz was out of the film industry because Babra had built a wall of hatred for him.

During her peak, Babra was charging up to Rs 300,000 for a film, but her demand dwindled due to the failure of a few films. Seeing the situation, Babra reduced her compensation from 300,000 to 121,000 Rupees.

In those days, Younis Malik was considered to be a successful director. Babra decided to trap him. Babra's cleverness worked and Younis Malik cast her in his film "Khoon Aur Pani."

The monthly "Shama-Lahore" wrote on page 98 of its January 1984 issue:

> "Khoon Aur Pani" was shot at Evernew Studio on Wednesday 23 November, 1983. That night Younis Malik filmed a disco song about Babra. At 1:00 AM, when the shooting was packed, Babra left in the car with Younis Malik. Their car was seen in the mini market of Gulberg at 3:00 AM where they were both busy in having a meal. After that, Younis Malik went to Babra's house to drop her off. The car entered the gate but did not come out because the main gate was closed. Nowadays, the love stories of Babra and

Younis are being talked about everywhere in the studio."

I think there is no need for any proof other than the above text because when the gate closes, the gate of desires is opened, from which the love drips drop by drop.

Babra Sharif and Ismail Shah

Ismail Shah was a handsome actor from Quetta city. Initially, he gave an excellent performance in a play titled "Shaheen," aired from PTV Karachi Center. After that he came to Lahore and started working in films. Mumtaz Ali Khan's "Baaghi Qaidi" was the debut film of Ismail Shah, which was released on 17 August 1980. Babra Sharif and Ismail teamed up in the film "Lady Smuggler," which was released on 7 August 1987. Both of them observed each other during the shooting of the film.

As Babra Sharif was quite a shrewd woman, she scrutinized Ismail Shah carefully. She realized that Ismail Shah was a penniless person and had very little financial resources and that Ismail Shah could not even bear her financial burden. That was why Babra was cautious. One important thing was that he was drunk all the time. But still, Babra spent time with him and assured him of her love. The news of their marriage was also in circulation in film circles in those days. But the relationship could not last for long.

Identity Card of Virgin Babra Sharif

Heroines are very fond of being called virgins in our film industry. Even if she becomes a mother of two or three children, she still pretends to be a virgin. Khushboo, Reema, Saima and Madiha Shah have children but they refuse to accept it.

Readers! You know that Shahid and Babra were officially married. In addition, she had relationships with Ilyas Kashmiri, Munawar Zarif, Shehzad Gul, Faisal, Ayaz, Ismail Shah, and sheikhs of the United Arab States, who all reached Babra Sharif's bedroom.

Why Did Babra Sharif Have to Pretend to Be a Virgin?

In fact, Babra Sharif was to visit India and meetings were also arranged with actor Dilip Kumar and other very important figures. No one in India knew whether Babra was married or a virgin. Also important was that she had to convince Dilip Kumar that she was completely untouched. So, Babra Sharif pretended to be a virgin by making an identity card. You can carefully look at Form A and B of the Identity Card which contains the following information.

Name Babra Sharif

Father's Name   Late Muhammad Sharif (Mr. Sharif had died at that time)

Address	House No. 45, G Block, Gulberg III.
Verifier	Tariq Latif Butt (who was then Manager of National Bank - Model Town). This meant that Babra was maintaining an account in the Model Town branch.
Date	1-1-89. That is, the form was filled on 89-1-1

Babra Sharif wrote her date of birth as 1964 on the form which is completely false. Actually, Babra Sharif was born in 1951 in the red-light district of Lahore. Babra's debut film "Intezar" was released in 1974. The film began to be produced in 1973 and Babra was 22 at that time according to her birth date of 1951. If the year of her birth is considered to be 1964, then in 1973 her age is calculated to be 9 years. This is impossible, because a 9-year-old girl cannot be a heroine, but a child star. This proved that she was 22 at the start of her first film.

There is a period of fifty years from 1951 to 2001, which is the actual age of Babra Sharif. Babra was 38 when she visited India. Therefore, it can be said that Babra traveled to India pretending to be a virgin at the age of 38 and because of this pretended virginity, she lured the high-profile people there. Even Dilip Kumar was a victim of her drama due to her pretended virginity.

Mohsin Hasan Khan and Babra Sharif

Mohsin Hasan Khan is a famous Pakistani ex-cricketer. A few years ago, he was a famous star in the world of cricket. He was married to Indian actress Reena Roy and fathered a daughter. He got a lot of fame due to his marriage to Reena Roy.

After marriage, Mohsin Khan and Reena Roy settled in Bombay. When Reena Roy broke her promise about working in films with Mohsin, he was deeply hurt and resented Reena Roy, he returned to Pakistan with his baby girl. After coming to Pakistan, he decided to act in films. He was cast as a hero against Babra in director Iqbal Yusuf's film "Raaz," which was released on July 17, 1992. It was during the shooting of the film that Babra and Mohsin became very close to each other.

Babra thought she had found another victim to pass the time. Therefore, she started using many tactics to overwhelm Mohsin. Mohsin fell into Babra's trap due to her tricks. On the other hand, Reena Roy in Bombay was also aware of the situation. She kept an eye on all the actions of Babra. She knew how many people Babra had ensnared before Mohsin. That love story could not be completed. However, Babra tried her best to get Mohsin Khan to marry her.

Mahmood Supra and Babra Sharif

Mahmood Supra was a rich and luxurious man. He used to associate with film stars. He also had a relationship with Salma Agha for a long time and even got engaged to her. But when he became cloyed with Salma Agha, he broke all ties with her. Mahmood Supra announced the production of a film "Khyber Horse" and at the same time he was planning to publish an English newspaper. As he was a favorite among film heroines, often actresses used to meet him. Babra Sharif also tried to get closer to Mahmood Supra and he made several false promises to her. Babra was already quite hurt, yet she chose to become close to Mahmood Supra. They also had a heated meeting in London. On there return to Pakistan, Mahmood approached Babra with a film script and roped her into the cast of his film. He told Babra that the film would be shot in the USA.

After that, Mahmood Supra took Babra to the USA so that she could see the location of the film. In America, Babra colored Mahmood Supra's many nights, and also brightened many days. Babra treated Mahmood with great love, which made him very happy.

Babra was sure that Mahmood would marry her in return for the colorful nights he had spent with her. After returning to Pakistan, Mahmood Supra also got the songs of the film recorded, but to date, he has not revealed those songs about Babra. After a few more days of revelry, he left Babra. Thus, Babra became alone again.

Babra's Mental State and Samaaj

As you know Babra Sharif has a long list of lovers but none of them stayed with her for life. Even her last victim Mahmood Supra escaped from her clutches. Her popularity in films also faded and many new girls like Resham, Saima, Meera, Noor and Reema etc. filled her place. Babra Sharif became an actress of the past. Even at the age of fifty, she does not accept agedness. She still considers herself young. A few years ago, when the actress Rani was alive, PTV approached Babra to act in the drama serial "Fareb," for which she demanded 200,000 Rupees per episode. That means PTV would have to pay Rs 2,600,000 for 13 episodes. PTV cast Rani in that drama serial instead, who did not even discuss compensation. The drama was very successful, which made Babra very sad.

1. All her lovers left Babra.
2. She stopped getting work in films.
3. New girls replaced Babra.

Thinking about the above things, she became very worried. She became irritated and stopped going out of the house. Some time ago, she also worked in a play called "Nadan Nadia" from PTV World, but that was not well received by the public, which gave her a further setback.

Those circumstances left Babra mentally paralyzed. Finally, she decided one day to join the camp of B.G., who is a dress designer. Nowadays, she is in demand by many filmmakers. B.G. and Babra made a plan together. According to the plan, Babra started visiting director Sangeeta's house. Sangeeta felt pity for Babra's mental state and a few days later, offered Babra a role in her film "Samaaj," which Babra accepted. Sangeeta, out of pity, had offered Babra a part in the film. But she had no idea what Babra was going to do with her in the next few days. On the occasion of the film's inauguration ceremony, B.G. called Sangeeta to tell her that Babra Sharif had ordered a dress worth 40,000 for the film and asked her to pay the bill immediately. Sangeeta was very sad to hear this and when she mentioned the phone call to filmmaker Sheikh Nazir Hussain, he told Sangeeta that he knew Babra Sharif very well, that she was a very clever woman and had done the same with him in director Waheed Dar's film "Ajab Khan." And that his film was delayed due to her dramatics. Later, both of them called B.G., suggesting that Babra could wear any dress for the function, and that 40,000 rupees would be paid later. Thus, Babra Sharif came to the ceremony and after the inauguration, Sangeeta paid Babra 40,000 rupees. Babra wore the same expensive dress and shot on the first day.

A few days later, another incident happened. Babra had not previously finalized her compensation for the film with Sangeeta. One day, Babra asked Sangeeta for the same compensation that Saima was receiving in those days. Filmmaker Sheikh Nazir got angry again. He said to Sangeeta that Babra had no market value and that she had been unnecessarily lenient with Babra.

However, Sheikh Nazir finalized the required compensation upon Sangeeta's request. By then, Sangeeta had recorded two songs for "Samaaj." Sangeeta informed Babra that the next schedule of film shooting would be 10 February, but Babra disappeared again on that occasion, causing Sangeeta a lot of trouble. In the meanwhile, Babra's secretary, named Zahoor, called Sangeeta to ask for 100,000 rupees to be sent to Babra Sharif in Karachi. Hearing that, Sangeeta got very angry and abused Babra that she had behaved like her lineal prostitutes. Later, Sangeeta contacted Sheikh Nazir Hussain, who said to her, "I already advised you to cut Babra from the film. Now suffer the consequences of not listening to me." Sangeeta told Sheikh Nazir that she had already spent 100,000 Rupees on the film and she would not be able to recover the loss. Mr. Shaikh said that he would compensate the loss and that Sangeeta should cut Babra from the film. Meanwhile, Sheikh Nazir took out 100,000 Rupees from a briefcase and gave it to Sangeeta and said that he would manage the remaining 60,000 rupees through the accounts of the distributors. Hearing that, Sangeeta cut Babra from the film. Babra's slyness with Sangeeta cost her dearly. She became mentally disturbed again and missed the chance to be in Sangeeta's film "Samaaj" in her late age.

A few days ago, some news broke out that Sangeeta had included the song filmed by Babra for Samaaj in her new film titled "Gharana." She further said that anyone who had any objections should compensate her and she would remove the song from the film.

Readers! You have read the story of Babra Sharif. Hope you have formed an opinion about Babra Sharif. I hope you will definitely inform me of this opinion.

Sangeeta

Kavita

MEHTAB BANO'S FAMILY

Sangeeta + Kavita

Sangeeta and Kavita are two famous actresses in the film world. In addition to acting, Sangeeta has also directed the films. Their mother, Mehtab Bano, played an important role in making them both busy actresses in the film industry. Their financial conditions were also similar to Babra Sharif's. Just as Babra's father Sharif used to make a living by selling ghee, Mehtab Bano was a nurse who barely managed the household expenses and lived in a modest quarter in Karachi, which rese mbled a hut. In addition to being a nurse, she sometimes performed the duties of a midwife. Mehtab Bano was a woman of modest appearance and did not have the slightest charm in her personality. She proved to be a virago by nature. Since she had a masculine body, she would beat anyone who misbehaved with her, in such a way that he would never come near her again. Many cases of such beatings are well known. For example, once a journalist wrote something wrong about Mehtab Bano and her daughters, so she invited the journalist to her home and beat him up, and the journalist did not dare do such a thing ever again.

Mehtab Bano also had a brother and a sister. Her sister was very beautiful and a good-looking lady with sharp features. She was married and died while giving birth to a beautiful baby girl. Mehtab Bano was a virgin at that time, so she adopted the girl and named her Parveen (Sangeeta).

It should be noted that Parveen was not the daughter of Mehtab Bano, but of her sister.

Mehtab Bano and Tayyab Rizvi

Tayyab Rizvi was a handsome young man. In the early days of his life, he used to sell tooth powder on the train. Later, he set up a small drug store. Mehtab Bano was very impressed by Tayyab Rizvi's beautiful personality. After a few great dates, the two willingly got married. Tayyab Rizvi was as upright mentally as he was good looking physically. He considered it his duty to obey everything his wife said. Mehtab often expressed to Tayyab Rizvi her desire to act in films.

On Mehtab Bano's insistence, Tayyab started working hard to introduce Mehtab into films. Eastern Studio was the only studio in Karachi in those days. Mehtab reached out to Eastern Studio with the help of Tayyab Rizvi.

Mehtab Bano lived in a small quarter at Lala Khet, which was located much farther from the studio. Due to her poor financial condition, Mehtab could not afford even a reasonable ride. But her passion was such that it became her daily routine to visit the filmmakers' offices. After a long stint, she only got the role of an extra, as she had no potential to become a heroine.

And yet It was not possible for her to abandon the dream of becoming a heroine. She was often present in the office of any of the filmmakers. One day, she reached out to the office of the director named Iqbal Yusuf, who was a young man and very gentle in the matter of women. So, soon enough the sounds of Mehtab's laughter started to be heard from Iqbal Yusuf's room.

Tayyab Rizvi also stopped coming to the studio with Mehtab as he could not close his drug shop every day. Mehtab used to leave the house alone in the morning to seduce Iqbal Yusuf for several hours. After going around the same offices, Mehtab became the mother of a girl named Nasreen (Kavita).

Ilyas Rasheedi and Mehtab Bano

There used to be a film journalist named Ilyas Rasheedi in Karachi, who was very popular and an influential person. He had close relations with the filmmakers. Apart from that, his weekly magazine "Nagar" was also quite popular. Shamim Ara, Ejaz and Zeba got into films with the help of Ilyas Rasheedi. Upon the insistence of her wife, Tayyab Rizvi somehow got access to Ilyas Rasheedi. Mr. Ilyas was an open-hearted man and the doors of his office were open to everyone. Tayyab and Mehtab used to visit Ilyas Rasheedi's office every day. It was

Mehtab Bano's routine that she went to Mr. Ilyas in the morning and would return home in the evening. One day, Ilyas Rasheedi advised Mehtab Bano to go to Lahore because it was the center of the film industry. Since this advice was sound, Mehtab quickly accepted it. But it was a problem to manage her fare for Lahore. She pleaded with Ilyas Rashidi that she did not even have the fare to go to Lahore. Mr. Ilyas not only arranged the fare but also referred her to some of the filmmakers and directors in Lahore.

Mehtab Bano's Family in Lahore

At that time, Parveen was about eight years old and Nasreen was an infant. After reaching Lahore, Mehtab Bano got a house on rent in a street of Nawan Kot. She also showed the reference letters to filmmakers that she had obtained from Ilyas Rasheedi. When they saw Mehtab Bano, they were shocked because she had no potential to be a heroine. In those days, a film titled "Koh-e Noor" was under production in which Sudheer and Zeba were playing the lead roles. Mehtab Bano managed to get the role for Parveen (Sangeeta) as a child star. That film, directed by Agha Hussaini, was released on 21 October 1966.

Time was passing and Mehtab Bano's hopes of becoming a heroine were fading. Once, Ilyas Rasheedi came to Lahore and Mehtab Bano cried in front of him. Ilyas Rasheedi explained to her that she should not waste her time and it would be better to go back to Karachi and start her own business. For Mehtab

Bano, going from Lahore to Karachi was a very humiliating moment, but fed up with the situation, she finally decided to go to Karachi. On reaching Karachi, Tayyab Rizvi took over his shop and Mehtab Bano started working as a midwife again.

Sangeeta and Rahman

After a few years, Sangeeta grew into a tall and beautiful lady. When Mehtab Bano saw Sangeeta's beauty, she thought of making Sangeeta a heroine and she took her to Ilyas Rasheedi's office. She pleaded to Mr. Rasheedi that even though she could not become a heroine but it would be a favor if her daughter could be made a film heroine. Ilyas Rasheedi promised that whenever a filmmaker had a role for a new girl, he would fulfill Mehtab's wish.

Rahman was a handsome actor. He lost one of his legs in an accident while shooting outdoors in East Pakistan. Rahman was very sad to lose his leg but still he did not give up and he managed to get a prosthetic leg. His acting was very popular in East Pakistan. Apart from that, he was also a flirtatious man and beautiful girls were his weakness.

When Rehman came to Karachi from East Pakistan and Ilyas Rasheedi told him about Sangeeta, he expressed his desire to meet Sangeeta. Mr. Rasheedi sent a message to Mehtab Bano to take Sangeeta to the hotel immediately. As soon as she got the message, Mehtab got Sangeeta to make up and reached the hotel. When Rahman saw Sangeeta's appearance, he was stunned. When Rahman explored Sangeeta thoroughly and was satisfied, he cast her in the film named "Kangan."

Thus, with the help of Ilyas Rasheedi, Sangeeta became the heroine of the film. Parveen's name was changed to Sangeeta for the film "Kangan." Rahman booked seats on PIA for Mehtab Bano's family. It was Mehtab Bano's first time traveling by plane, so her joy was evident. Director Rehman's movie "Kangan" was released on 15 August 1969. "Kangan" turned out to be an average film. Had the film become a super hit, Mehtab Bano's days would have changed. After Sangeeta became a heroine, Mehtab Bano left Karachi again and came to Lahore.

Shammi Malik and Sangeetha

Shammi Malik was a filmmaker, who produced only a few films, including "Ghairat Mand" and "Do Badan" etc. Shammi Malik was fond of women and the girls from the red-light district were his mistresses at different times. Famous actress Zamurd had been his mistress for monthly wages. When Sangeeta came to Lahore and did not get any film, she also started looking for a wealthy man. In the beginning, Sangeeta became the mistress of Ilyas Kashmiri. In those days, Shammi Malik got angry with Zamurd. The reason was that Zamurd was very flirtatious and befriended almost everyone. Apart from others, the actress was also having an affair with Shahid, so she was not giving proper time to Shammi Malik. Shammi Malik kept Sangeeta with him for monthly wages to make Zamurd feel jealous – thus Sangeeta got a livelihood in Lahore.

Sangeeta and Iqbal Hassan

Sangeeta now started getting supporting roles in films. Since in those days Zeba, Deeba, Rani, Rozeena, Shabnam and Shamim were ruling the film industry in Lahore as heroines, Sangeeta acted as a supporting actress in films including "Salam-e-Mohabbat," "Chand Sooraj," "Chiragh Kahan, Roshni Kahan," "Yeh Aman," "Khalish," "Ilzam" and "Naag Mony."

Iqbal Hassan and Sangeeta featured together for the first time in Riaz Shahid's film "Yeh Aman." The film was released on November 20, 1971. Actor Iqbal Hasan was slightly stubborn in nature and often used to have petty quarrels. There was also a masculine element in him and Mehtab Bano needed such a man to protect herself and Sangeeta. So, Sangeeta befriended Iqbal Hassan who took her to a beautiful house. He also used to feed Sangeeta a breakfast of Siri Pai every morning from Yasin's Hotel in Royal Park and was also trying to get roles for Sangeeta in more films. But the relationship did not last long. I will explain the reasons for this in the following pages. Iqbal Hassan worked mostly in Punjabi films. He also played the title role in "Sher Khan" which was released on August 2, 1981 and became a success.

Sangeetha and Ijaz Durrani

Actor Ijaz Durrani needs no introduction and has long been the handsome hero of his era in the film industry. Along with acting, he also produced films. When Ijaz was in the field of acting, many film actresses were inclined towards him, including Firdous, Naghma, Saloni and Noor Jahan etc. Later, Noor Jahan also got married to Ijaz.

The actress Sangeeta also fell in love with Ijaz Durrani to which Ijaz too responded with love. Sangeeta also opened the doors of her house for Ijaz to develop a relationship with her, but in those days Ijaz was sandwiched between Noor Jahan and Firdous. He could not give much time to Sangeeta, so their romantic story could go no further.

Sangeeta's Film History

Sangeeta acted as the heroine at the age of 13 in Rahman's film "Kangan," though she had earlier acted as a child star in "Koh-e-Noor." Sangeeta acted in Urdu and Punjabi films.

Some of Sangeeta's Best Films as an Actress

Title of Film	Language	Director	Release Date
Kangan	Urdu	Rehman	15-Aug-1969
Khushiya	Punjabi	Haider Chaudhry	16-Nov-1973
Chakar Baz	Urdu	S. Jamsheri	13-Dec-1974
Society Girl	Urdu	Sangeeta	16-Apr-1976

Mohabbat Aur Mehangai	Urdu	Iqbal Rizvi	6-Aug-1976
Mujhey Galey Laga Lou	Urdu	Sangeeta	22-Oct-1976
Ishque	Urdu	Sangeeta	14-Jul-1977
Susral	Urdu	Nazar Shabab	28-Oct-1977
Muthi Bhar Chawal	Urdu	Sangeeta	16-Jun-1978
Mere Sapnoun ka Mehal	Urdu	Sangeeta	21-Mar-1980
Raka	Punjabi	Mumtaz Ali Khan	11-Jul-1983
Sona Chandi	Punjabi	Rangeela	18-Sep-1983
Qismat	Punjabi	Iqbal Kashmiri	20-Jun-1985
Mehandi	Punjabi	Altaf Hussain	1-Nov-1985

Sangeetha and Shahid

While writing the story of Babra Sharif, I told you that I would write the story of Shahid and Sangeeta in the coming pages. As you know, Shahid was a womanizer and women were also very attracted to him. Similarly, Sangeeta's attention also turned towards Shahid. They first appeared together in Aziz ul Hasan's film "Dill Ka Shehar" which was released on June 1, 1973. In those days, Shahid was married to Zamurd, but still Sangeeta's beautiful body attracted Shahid. Both of them kept having love-meetings in secret from Emerald. Both started appearing together in films as well. Some are listed on the next page.

Title of Film	Language	Director	Release Date
Baharoun ki Manzil	Urdu	S. Suleman	21-Dec-1973
Ustaad	Punjabi	Wazir Ali	25-Apr-1975
Sindbad	Urdu	Iqbal Kashmiri	25-Apr-1975
Balounat Kaur	Punjabi	M. Saleem Ahmed	17-Oct-1975
Wardaat	Punjabi	Diljit Mirza	4-Jun-1976

Shahid left Sangeeta along with other women after his relationship with Babra Sharif in 1976. Sangeeta had been in love with actor Muhammad Ali for a few days, but Zeba overpowered him in time and dashed Sangeeta's hopes.

Sangeetha as Director

When the Pakistani film industry did not accept Sangeeta as a heroine, Mehtab Bano thought of bringing her into the field of directing. She believed that Sangeeta would do well in the field of directing. Sangeeta herself was very clever and smart so she decided to make film directing her future, in order to stay in the film world.

In this regard, Sangeeta released her debut film, titled "Society Girl," as a director. The film was very successful and the film world recognized Sangeeta as a director. Sangeeta has directed many films to date, some of which even celebrated a golden jubilee like "Society Girl," "Ishque," "Mujhe Gale Laga Lou," "Muthi Bhar Chawal" and "Mahal Mere Sapnoun Ka," making Sangeeta one of the best directors. Apart from these, a few more films are listed on the next page.

Title of Film	Release Date	Successful / Flop	Award
Mera Naam Badnaam	4-May-19	Successful	Nigar Award
Jeene Nahi Doon Gi	26-Jul-1985	Successful	Nigar Award
Khilouna	1-Nov-1996	Successful	Nigar Award
Nikah	5-Jun-1998	Successful	Nigar Award
Sultana Daku	11-Aug-2000	Successful	
Gharana	11-May-2001	Flop	

All the above films became Sangeetha's signature films. Owing to these films, Sangeeta is still in the field of directing. Her last successful film was "Sultana Daku," which did business even during crisis days. Apart from these films, Sangeeta also directed "Qasam Munne Ki", "Tezab", "Shehanshah", Zeharile, Dou Boond Pani, Dream Girl, Ehsaas, Qismat, Harjai, Gharana and "Reshmaan".

Sangeeta and Humayun Qureshi

Although Sangeeta started directing, she did not stop acting even after becoming a successful director. Wealth was coming to her house from both sides, but Sangeeta had no legal rights to that wealth. All the money was being deposited in Mehtab Bano's account. She would get money only for daily expenses. Sangeeta also never made any demands from her mother in terms of money.

Many years passed and Sangeeta entered middle age. Her face also began to show aging effects. She had also started wearing spectacles. Mehtab and Tayyab were seeing all the physical changes of Sangeeta but they were not worried about Sangeeta's marriage. So, what would Sangeeta herself say?

In the same days, a new young man named Humayun Qureshi came from Frontier Province into the film world. He started his career with a Pashto film titled "Kallah Khizan, Kallah Bahar." He was very much in love with Sangeeta but never expressed his love. He mentioned his love to actress Musarrat Shaheen because she was considered quite an expert in developing peoples' relationships. In those days, Musarrat Shaheen and actress Yasmin Khan were friends of Sangeeta. Musarrat Shaheen promised Humayun Qureshi that she would convince Sangeeta. One day, Musarrat Shaheen talked about Humayun casually and later both Musarrat and Yasmeen started praising Humayun regularly. They started telling Sangeeta, "Humayun cannot live without you. If you reject him, he will lose his life. He sees the image of his ideal in with you. You are the only person in the world who can make him happy."

Both of them said the above things to Sangeeta because they were aware of the situation in Sangeeta's house.One day they went to Humayun Qureshi's house with Sangeeta, who was surprised to see her photographs displayed on the walls in every room. Now she was convinced that Humayun Qureshi really loved her immensely. Long story short, Musarrat and Yasmeen convinced Sangeeta to marry Humayun Qureshi.

They both set up a secret program that Mehtab and Tayyab did not know about. Sangeeta and Humayun Qureshi's Nikah was solemnized in the presence of a few close ones during the outdoor shooting of the film "Sohni Surat." When the news of the Nikah reached Mehtab Bano, she felt very bad, but nothing could be done at that time.

Mehtab and Tayyab did not speak to Sangeeta for several days, but later on they quelled their anger on their own. After a year, a baby girl was born to Sangeeta and thus a strong relationship was established between Humayun Qureshi and Sangeeta, which made Mehtab Bano very sad.

Mehtab and Tayyab planned to take revenge on Sangeeta. When Sangeeta became successful as a director, Mehtab and Tayyab formed a personal film production company registered in Sangeeta's name which was being managed by Tayyab Rizvi. For many years, Income Tax Department notices were being issued in Sangeeta's name, but instead of paying the tax, Tayyab Rizvi got the notices canceled by paying bribes. The name of that company was PNR Production.

Tayyab Rizvi earned millions of rupees through that company. Sangeeta had never inquired about the company and was living separately with her husband. She was sure that Tayyab Rizvi was doing well. But when Sangeeta came to know about the situation, she became very worried because a tax bill amounting to 8 million Rupees was due for that company. In other words, her father Tayyab Rizvi had had embezzled 8 million Rupees.

After the birth of the baby girl, Sangeeta's body shape was not the same as before. She also started using thick spectacles instead of thin ones. For Humayun Qureshi, she was now an ordinary woman as she had lost all her charm. Mehtab Bano was also misleading Humayun Qureshi about Sangeeta. On the other hand, Humayun Qureshi did not like Sangeeta's liberty. All such circumstances created a rift between them, and eventually they got divorced.

A few years after the divorce, Humayun Qureshi became a famous villain. His famous films include "Sher Dill," "Putar Jagge Da," "Machh Jail," "Sharaft," "Achhu 302," "Khuda Gawah," "Zabardast," "Paani," "Kaale Chour," "Madam Bawri," "Gujjar Badshah," "Asmaan" and "Insaniyat ke Dushman" etc.

It should be noted that their daughter stayed with Sangeeta who got her married and has now become a maternal grandmother.

Sangeetha and Shahbaz Akmal

Shahbaz Akmal, son of the past actor Muhammad Akmal (late), was a handsome young man. He decided to try his luck in the film industry after the death of his father. Shahbaz Akmal's debut film was "Dill Maa Da," featuring Sangeeta alongside him. The film, directed by Muhammad Salim, was released on 23 November 1984.

Seeing the beauty of Shahbaz Akmal, it seemed that Muhammad Akmal had become young again. Sangeeta was feeling lonely after getting divorced from Humayun Qureshi and was looking for an attachment to keep herself busy. Suddenly she noticed Shahbaz Akmal. Those days, Sangeeta was praising Shahbaz Akmal everywhere and on the other hand, Shahbaz was also seen praising Sangeeta whilst in the company of his friends. They both wished that the director would cast both of them together in the film. A few filmmakers and directors honored their wishes and even cast the two together.

The two worked together in the following films.

Title of Film	Director	Release Date
Dill Maan Da	Muhammad Saleem	23-Nov-1984
Shikra	Zahoor Hussain	20-Jun-1985
Kaffara	Younis Rathor	14-Feb-1986
Nishan	Altaf Hussain	4-Jul-1986
Laali Badshah	Raja Imtiaz	28-Nov-1986

The relationship of Sangeeta and Shahbaz did not last long as Shahbaz Akmal, as handsome as he was, did not turn out to be as good a hero according to Sangeeta's expectations. So, that relationship was not built on sincerity but on a transactional basis.

Sangeeta's Second Marriage

After some time of being divorced, the desire to remarry arose in Sangeeta's heart. At that time, Sangeeta's personality was not as attractive as before. Although She was getting old, her emotions were still young. When she looked around for a reasonable person, she saw a handsome man in the form of Naveed Akbar Butt. Seeing him, Sangeeta felt as if she had received support for her old age. So, after a few ordinary meetings, Sangeeta formally got married to Naveed Akbar Butt. Naveed Akbar Butt was quite a wealthy person. Initially, he was a car dealer, but afterwards he became involved in film making with Sangeeta. Below are some of Naveed Akbar Butt's films that were directed by Sangeeta.

Title of Film	Release Date
Khilona	1-Nov-1996
Ashqui Khel Nahin	18-Apr-1997
Qaid	12-May-2000
Reshman	12-May-2000

Naveed Akbar Butt and Sangeeta's married life was going very well until one day they had a fight. Someone published a cheap scandal about Sangeeta in a newspaper, and as soon as it was published, Sangeeta started receiving telephone calls from all over the country. Even his son-in-law asked the reason for the scandal. Sangeeta panicked at the situation and took sleeping pills. With great difficulty, doctors were able to save her life.

After being discharged from the hospital, Sangeeta held a press conference and blamed her husband Naveed Akbar Butt for publishing false scandals about her and falsely accusing her as well as her daughters. She said Naveed Akbar was a lazy man who had not done any work for the last ten years and was using shameless language against her first daughter. She said that her daughter was the mother of three daughters and six months pregnant.

She further blamed Naveed of wanting to deprive her daughter of her right to property and that he had also made a murderous attack on her. And that her and her daughters' lives were not safe, so she was going to move her daughters to USA. After the press conference, a bitter conversation started between Naveed Akbar Butt and Sangeeta, which ended in the form of divorce between both. After the divorce, she moved to the USA.

Kavita

As Nasreen (Kavita) transitioned from her childhood to adulthood, her beauty caused an apocalypse. Her sharp features were dazzling the eyes of the viewers. Whenever Mehtab took Kavita to the studio with her, she would gather a crowd around her with her swagger, audacity and frankness. As Kavita's beauty was considerably high, she could not handle it.

Mehtab Bano often did not allow Kavita to go out of the house. Instead, she locked the house and went out. But Kavita would still get out through the window. Seeing her beautiful appearance, Mehtab Bano started efforts to make her an actress.

Entering the Film World

In the previous pages, I mentioned actor Iqbal Hasan's friendship with Mehtab Bano and Sangeeta. Iqbal Hasan used to visit their house a lot. One of the major flaws in Mehtab Bano was that she was foul-mouthed. She did not respect anyone and became rude to others without thinking.

Due to such habits, one day in the studio, Mehtab Bano used very bad language about Iqbal Hasan, which Iqbal Hasan's friends informed him about. Hearing all that, Iqbal Hasan got angry and went to their house. Luckily, both of them were not present at home. After Iqbal Hasan's departure, when Mehtab Bano reached her house, the servants told her that Iqbal Hasan was very angry and had threatened to kidnap Kavita. As fighting was a trivial matter for Iqbal Hasan, Sangeeta and Mehtab Bano became scared.

Next day early in the morning, Mehtab Bano reached Shammi Malik's house. Due to fear, Kavita and Sangeeta were also with their mother. In those days, Sangeeta was Shammi Malik's mistress because he had broken up with Zamurd. Shammi Malik was surprised to see them. He promised Mehtab that he would cool down Iqbal Hasan and after their departure, he did so. But Mehtab Bano was still scared. She pleaded Shammi Malik to give Kavita a chance in films by any means.

Shammi Malik was planning to produce a film titled "Dou Badan" in those days. So, he cast Kavita in the film to end Mehtab Bano's fear and to form a strong friendship with

Sangeeta. Thus, with Mehtab Bano's best planning, Kavita became a film star. This film, directed by Razzak, was released on 5 January 1974. Apart from Kavita, Nadeem and Shabnam played the lead roles. The film was a flop.

Some Famous Movies of Kavita

Kavita mostly acted in Sangeeta's films. She worked in fewer films with other directors. I will explain the reason in the following pages.

URDU FILMS

Title of Film	Director	Release Date
Tere Mere Sapnay	Iqbal Rizvi	16-May-1975
Aurat Aik Paheli	Jaffar Bukhari	26-Mar-1976
Society Girl	Sangeeta	16-Apr-1976
Mohabbat Aur Mehangai	Iqbal Rizvi	6-Aug-1976
Mujhey Galay Laga Lou	Sangeeta	22-Oct-1976
Ishque	Sangeeta	14-Jul-1977
Laad Pyar Aur Beti	Sangeeta	19-May-1978
Maen Chup Rahun Gi	Sangeeta	18-May-1979
Laad Aandhi	Sangeeta	29-Jun-1979
Mian Bivi Raazi	Sangeeta	29-Jan-1982
Mera Naam Badnaam	Sangeeta	4-May-1984
Jeene Nahi Doon Gi	Sangeeta	26-Jul-1985
Manila Ki Bijliyan	Jaan Muhammad	29-May-1987
Arood Ki Chhaoun Mein	Nazar Islam	18-Aug-1989
Jangju Goreelay	Aziz Tabbasum	27-Apr-1990
Aalmi Jasoos	Jaan Muhammad	16-Apr-1991

PUNJABI FILMS

Title of Film	Director	Release Date
Sher Baz Khan	Hassan Askari	21-Oct-1988
Badshah	Zahoor Hussain Gilani	9-Jun-1989
Daket	Jahangir Qaiser	23-Jun-1989
Paani	Haider Chaudhry	6-Oct-1989
Mujrim	Haider Chaudhry	22-Dec-1989
Siren	M. Aslam	7-Dec-1996
Qatil Qaidi	Khalifa Saeed Ahmed	13-Sep-1991
Hijrat	Shahid Rana	12-Jun-1992

You have seen the above list of famous movies of Kavita. In all these films, the glimpse of Kavita's beauty is evident. After working for a few years, when Kavita came to know how to work in the films, she also resorted to sex like other heroines. You can see Kavita's sex scenes in the movie "Manila Ki Bijilyan" and "Aalmi Jasoos."

After Urdu films, when Kavita started acting in Punjabi films, she took her boldness to another level. Her scenes in "Badshah Dakait," "Hoshiyar," "Mujrim" and "Khuda Baksh" made moviegoers flock to the cinema. Kavita's fighting scenes in these films were also worth watching. During the fighting scenes, she would rotate her legs in such a way that the audience would forget the whole movie and prefer to watch only her fight scenes.

Haider Chaudhry's "Paani" is a film in which Kavita is seen at the height of sex. Tayyab Rizvi watched this movie sitting in the cinema with Kavita. When he could not bear the boldness of his daughter, he put his hands over his eyes in shame. It can be said that he became extremely embarrassed after seeing "Pani."

Two Hundred Thousand and Kavita

Like other heroines, Kavita actively also participated in non-film activities. Most of her victims were rich, noblemen and ministers.

One of Kavita's non-film deals went something like this. This was in those days when she had just entered adulthood. A famous 55-year-old witch doctor Safi ud Din had attended a gathering arranged by Maulana Kausar Niazi. When Safi ud Din saw Kavita, he fell in love with her. He asked Maulana Kausar Niazi to arrange his meeting with Kavita as soon as possible. Maulana Kausar Niazi mentioned his eagerness to Mehtab Bano who said to Mr. Maulana to stay out of the deal, and that she would please Mr. Safi ud Din herself.

Mehtab Bano demanded that Mr. Safi ud Din pay 100,000 for Kavita's first meeting and he immediately agreed to it. But seeing his eagerness, Mehtab increased the amount from 100,000 to 200,000, which Mr. Safi ud Din gladly paid.

Seeing Kavita's boldness and antics, Mr. Safi ud Din was trapped in her tricks for a lifetime. Then often he would resort to Kavita's body to end his indecisiveness. His indecisiveness did not end but Kavita became the mother of a baby girl. After the birth of the baby girl, he built a beautiful house for Kavita.

Kavita's daughter was born almost twenty years before the incident was recorded. Mehtab Bano said that she was the mother of the baby girl, but her appearance did not match Kavita. That beautiful girl looked exactly like Mr. Safi ud Din. This lie of Mehtab's could not fool people.

As long as Mr. Safi ud Din lived, he continued to present all the offerings of his devotion in the service of Kavita. He stopped Kavita from acting in films for a long time. With great difficulty, he agreed to allow Kavita to act only in Sangeeta's films. Because he would have given Mehtab Bano so much money that she would have either refused the filmmakers or would have asked for such a high compensation to work in Kavita's film that the filmmakers would have turned back. As soon as Mr. Safi ud Din died, Kavita started signing up for films in droves.

Diamond Trader and Kavita

A few years ago, a handsome young diamond merchant came to Mehtab Bano. He said that he had a lot of money and wanted to produce a film in Pakistan. Mehtab Bano gave him a chance to come close to Kavita. After a few days, Mehtab Bano realized that his intentions were different and that the man might elope with Kavita. She imposed restrictions on Kavita, but the young man did not stop chasing Kavita. Whenever he went on business tours to Bangkok, Japan and Hong Kong, he would present beautiful diamonds to Kavita on his return. Once, Kavita also planned to elope with the man but Mehtab Bano did not let their plan succeed.

A Young Man from Shikarpur

Kavita mostly traveled by plane, and whenever a film of Sangeeta was stopped by the censor, Kavita would take a flight to Islamabad and on her return flight she would have the certificate of the censor board in her hand and the film would be cleared.

During these trips, she once fell in love with a young man from Shikarpur. Kavita and he kept meeting secretly but Mehtab Bano got word of their love and imposed strict restrictions on Kavita. Kavita kept in touch with the man by telephone, but this also came to the knowledge of Mehtab Bano.

Finally fed up, Kavita tried to commit suicide by taking sleeping pills. Mehtab Bano came to know about the suicide attempt in time and immediately took Kavita to the hospital. Thus, she became an obstacle in the way of Kavita's suicide.

Mehtab Bano is a very clever woman and she can count the wings of a flying bird. She knows a lot about her daughters and their every move is in her knowledge. She was also known to have a spell by which she could find out the status of her daughters. But that magic did not work when Sangeeta secretly married Humayun Qureshi.

Nowadays, Kavita has left the film industry. She has been residing in America and sometimes visits Pakistan. Mr. Safi ud Din's daughter also lives with her.

Kavita is now more than 40 years old but still looks very beautiful. A few days ago, there was news that Kavita got married to a Sikh, but then this news was denied. Sometimes it is said she had opened a boutique in USA. Once there was another story that Kavita had opened a hotel in the USA.

Whatever the case may be, Kavita remains in Pakistani newspapers and continues to make her presence felt.

Musarrat Shaheen

MUSARRAT SHAHEEN

From Showbiz to Politics

A fair complexion, height 5 feet 6 inches, an extremely young, sexy girl, bold, fearless and always smiling – this lady's name is Musarrat Shaheen. She achieved equal popularity in Urdu, Punjabi and Pashto films. Musarrat Shaheen acted in films for 22 years and now she is showing her talent in the field of politics.

The Beginning

Musarrat Shaheen was born in 1954 in Dera Ismail Khan. Her mother tongue is Saraiki and her education is F.A. She was born to a very poor family; her father was a truck driver and her mother was a midwife. Her father died early and her mother had to bear the burden of Musarrat Shaheen and three other sisters alone. Poverty camped in their house. Seeing the situation, Musarrat Shaheen became very worried. She moved to Lahore and started cabaret dancing at the Flatties Hotel in Lahore. Najma, Romani and Chakori also used to dance in that hotel. Chakori is the sister of the famous dress designer

B.G. – later she changed her name from Chakori to Shabana Sheikh. Thus Musarrat Shaheen, Najma, Romani and Chakori created a sensation with their dances at the Flatties Hotel. Musarrat Shaheen used to display her body under colorful lights every night and would delight the customers by wearing a short dress. The hotel owners used to collect a lot of money from the customers but only gave a small commission to Musarrat Shaheen, which did not improve her financial position. One of her fans advised her to publish her sexy photos in magazines to gain fame. Accepting the advice, she started making sexy poses for magazines. All the salacious magazines of 1973–74 continued to publish bold pictures of Musarrat Shaheen.

Due to these pictures, Musarrat Shaheen gained a lot of popularity. Then one day after seeing those pictures, a filmmaker offered her a role in the film "Ajj Di Gall." The director of that film was Asad Bukhari and the film was released on May 2, 1975. She was still working on the film when Mumtaz Ali Khan gave her a chance in his film "Dulhan Aik Raat Ki," which was released on 12 December 1975. The success of this film made Musarrat famous all over Pakistan. The film, in which Musarrat Shaheen did some very sexy dances, celebrated the Diamond Jubilee. That film is still preserved in the mind of moviegoers. Thus, Musarrat Shaheen started getting work in films and her days of poverty were over.

The hardships of her life had made Musarrat Shaheen smart, fearless, bold and a woman who worked like men. She had innumerable love affairs, most of which were based on selfishness, because she had seen a lot of poverty since her childhood. Money was her greatest weakness; she considered her body as a toy. Whenever she wanted, she would take money and hand over her body. She felt no shame in doing so as her desires were fulfilled in the form of money. Let us discuss some of her friends.

Muhammad Afzal and Musarrat Shaheen

This man from Rawalpindi was a marble merchant. One day he met Musarrat Shaheen at a party. When Musarrat Shaheen discovered that Muhammad Afzal was a wealthy person, she stuck with him. Seeing Musarrat Shaheen's sexy body, Muhammad Afzal could not control himself either. The two continued to meet in different hotels and secret corners of the studio. Musarrat Shaheen pleased Muhammad Afzal openly, which impressed him a lot and one day he got emotional and proposed to her. Musarrat Shaheen's ears were already eager to hear his proposal. She accepted it with a few conditions, which Muhammad Afzal fulfilled and gifted her a house in Gulbarg, a car and a large bank balance.

After taking the above items, Musarrat Shaheen married Muhammad Afzal. After marriage, she traveled to many countries on the pretext of honeymooning. In those countries, she also did shopping worth millions of rupees with Muhammad Afzal's money. Muhammad Afzal, being a victim of Musarrat's seduction, would have done everything that she asked for. He had no power left to think and would only follow Musarrat's orders. Musarrat Shaheen was very happy at the foolishness of her victim.

When Musarrat Shaheen got fed up with Afzal, she started quarreling with him. In this conflict, one day she pushed Muhammad Afzal out of the house and seized all his property. After that, Musarrat approached the court for divorce and got the divorce from Afzal through advocate Safdar Javed Cheema. Thus, with this plan, Musarrat Shaheen was able to grab a lot of property.

Safdar Javed Cheema and Musarrat Shaheen

Safdar Javed Cheema played an important role in getting Musarrat Shaheen divorce from Muhammad Afzal. Instead of paying the fee to Safdar Javed, Musarrat kept him engaged in revelry with her. Their relationship became so popular in the film studio that news of their marriage started appearing in the newspapers, but Musarrat denied the news.

For some time, Musarrat pretended to be in love with Safdar Javed Cheema, but as soon as she saw a new victim, she broke up with him. Safdar Javed was left empty-handed; he neither received the case fee nor enjoyed Musarrat Shaheen's intimacy. The love affair ended after only a few stories were published in the newspapers and a few days of intimate gossip.

Shahid Akbar Awan and Musarrat Shaheen

Shahid Akbar Awan was a handsome young man and his elder brother Khalid Akbar Awan, was a distributor of English films in Royal Park, Lahore, while his family resided in Sargodha.

How Did Shahid Akbar Awan Meet Musarrat Shaheen?

The details are as follows: the actress Waheeda Khan's brothers were to perform a play titled "Naqli Biwi" at Sargodha's Shaheen Cinema. Waheeda Khan was a friend of Musarrat Shaheen and on the insistence of her brothers, she asked Musarrat Shaheen to attend her play as a special guest. Musarrat Shaheen accepted Waheeda Khan's request because of their relationship and inaugurated the play on 29 July, 1980. Due to her arrival, many people watched the play and for every show, the house was full. On the second day, Musarrat Shaheen was to return to Lahore, but the owner of the cinema, Khalid Akbar Awan wanted Musarrat Shaheen to stay on the second day as well, but she refused.

When Khalid's brother Shahid Akbar Awan saw the situation, he decided to meet Musarrat Shaheen himself. When Shahid met Musarrat, he invited her to dinner after a formal conversation. Musarrat Shaheen accepted the invitation and had a sumptuous dinner with Shahid. Musarrat Shaheen stayed in Sargodha at Shahid's insistence. Due to Musarrat's presence in the drama, the management earned millions.

Shahid Akbar Awan also took the address of Musarrat Shaheen's house so that he could go to Lahore and continue the chain of meetings with her. A few days later, under this plan, Shahid went to Lahore and had a meeting with Musarrat Shaheen. Now Shahid made it a routine that whenever Musarrat Shaheen went to Karachi for shooting, Shahid Akbar would come to Karachi. He was present at every one of Musarrat Shaheen's film sets.

There was a lot of talk about their story in the newspapers, but Musarrat Shaheen denied it. A few months later, Shahid Akbar Awan and Musarrat Shaheen also went on a world tour in December 1980. On their return, they were planning to get married. When Shahid's parents got to know the whole story, they scolded Shahid, asking why he was hanging out with a dancer, and that he should be ashamed as he belonged to a respected family and should not dishonor his elders in that way. Shahid's parents further said that if he married Musarrat, they would deprive him of their property.

After the insult, Shahid Akbar made a firm promise to his parents that he would never meet Musarrat Shaheen again. Since Musarrat Shaheen had spent many colorful nights with Shahid Akbar, she did not step back and give up. She had her eye on Shahid Akbar's property and cinema to somehow get both.

Having this desire, when Masarrat Shaheen met Shahid, he said that he could not deny his parents for her. He asked Musarrat if she would give him 1,500,000 Rupees to leave his parents. He said that it was her minimal condition and if Musarrat would accept the condition, he would abandon his parents for her. On the other hand, Musarrat was also waiting to get married to Shahid quickly so that she could take over his property.

Finally, one day they got married secretly. It was only a short time after the wedding that Musarrat Shaheen started making demands on Shahid Akbar. Since Shahid was quite a smart man, he did not fulfill any big demands. Meanwhile, Shahid's parents were also insisting that he should divorce her. Musarrat felt that the plan to grab his property was going to fail, so she separated from Shahid and found a way to escape. But Shahid did not divorce Musarrat and also hid the marriage certificate. Musarrat made many efforts to get the marriage certificate but all her efforts were in vain.

Imtiaz Ahmed Cheema and Musarrat Shaheen

When Musarrat Shaheen got nothing from Shahid Akbar Awan, she started looking for a new victim. At last, a landlord from Sargodha named Imtiaz Ahmad Cheema met her. Musarrat surrendered herself to Imtiaz to cement her relationship. In that way, Imtiaz Ahmed became the companion of Musarrat's solitude.

Musarrat Shaheen also wanted the victim to come into the cage somehow. Since she had already done a lot of research about Imtiaz and his property details, she was getting closer to him day by day. Her relationship blossomed and one day, Imtiaz

Ahmad Cheema married her. She requested a new bungalow from Imtiaz.

Imtiaz said to Musarrat, "You are already living in the bungalow." In response, Musarrat said that the bungalow was outdated and that she would live in the new bungalow with Imtiaz. After that answer, Imtiaz Ahmed Cheema bought Musarrat a new bungalow and after few days, she moved into it. It was only a few days after moving into the new bungalow that Musarrat sold the old bungalow so that she could easily occupy the new one. But her plan remained a dream, as Imtiaz had bought the new bungalow in his own name. Musarrat thought that she would evict Imtiaz from the bungalow like Mohammad Afzal, but it remained only a wish and could not be reality.

On the other hand, a new situation arose. It so happened that someone told Imtiaz Cheema that Musarrat Shaheen had not got a formal divorce from Shahid Akbar Awan but had only separated – that is, Musarrat Shaheen had entered into another marriage while already being married, which was illegitimate according to Sharia.

Those circumstances were unbearable for Musarrat Shaheen and she could not dodge and get rid of Imtiaz Cheema. She knew that if the matter went to court, she would be in trouble. So, she thought it best to remain silent and happily lived with Imtiaz Cheema and a year later, she also gave birth to a beautiful baby girl.

Musarrat Shaheen as an Actress

Musarrat Shaheen has achieved many successes as an actress. She acted in Urdu, Punjabi and Pashto films. Initially she used to dance in films, but later she got the status of a heroine. When she started acting in Pashto films, nudity and obscenity became common in the films. Whatever film Musarrat Shaheen would perform in, there would be obscenity in it.

Musarrat Shaheen's debut film "Ajj Di Gall" was not a big success, but her second film "Dulhan Aik Raat Ki" set records of success. In that film, Musarrat Shaheen, Nimmi and Suraya Khan danced so beautifully and excitingly that people started getting emotional and engaged in doing strange acts in the cinema hall. The girls were dressed in such skinny and skimpy clothes that their bodies seemed to be coming.

Similarly, director Saeed Ali Khan's film "Gringo," which was released on July 14, 1989, was very successful because of Musarrat Shaheen's nudity. Whoever saw "Gringo" was shocked to see such nudity. Rather, there were some scenes that surpassed even Indian and English films. Musarrat Shaheen was in and she filmed such scenes in the film that viewers became stunned. In a song shot in the rain, she took it to the extreme. About which I have no words to write.

Musarrat Shaheen acted in many films from 1975 to 1997. Let us see a list of a few of her films.

Title of Film	Language	Director	Release Date
Dulhan Aik Raat Ki	Urdu	Mumtaz Ali Khan	12-Dec-1975
Mohabbat Aur Dosti	Urdu	Khalifa Saeed Ahmed	15-Oct-1976
Cheekh	Urdu	Iqbal Bhatti	4-Aug-1977
Amber	Urdu	Nazar Islam	6-Jan-1978
Chugha	Pashto	Yousaf Bhatti	22-Feb-1978
Accident	Punjabi	Haider Chaudhry	14-Jul-1978
Multan Khan	Urdu	Salma Mumtaz	13-Jul-1979
Gehray Zakham	Urdu	Mumtaz Ali Khan	3-Nov-1979
Zakhmuna	Pashto	Mumtaz Ali Khan	30-May-1980
Navay Aunkrezay	Pashto	Waheeda Khan	9-Oct-1980
Bangri Aur Hathkari	Pashto	Mumtaz Ali Khan	4-Feb-1983
Murad Khan	Punjabi	Waheed Dar	12-Aug-1983
Shikari	Urdu	Mumtaz Ali Khan	17-Feb-1984
Gringu	Pashto	Saeed Ali Khan	14-Jul-1989
Da Dushman Inteqam	Pashto	Munir Khan	8-Nov-1991
Sari Khor	Pashto	Saeed Ali Khan	3-Mar-1995
Gul Badan	Pashto	Irfan Saeed	13-Sep-1996

The above list of films shows that Musarrat Shaheen worked in Urdu, Punjabi and Pashto films, in which the name of the famous director of Urdu films, Nazar Islam, also appears.

She also introduced her younger sister Sawera into films, whose debut film was "Zara Si Baat," directed by Nazar Shabab. Sawera could not meet the demands of the big screen and hence was soon out of films.

Musarrat Shaheen also tried to direct the films in addition to acting. She released "Baat Ban Jaye" as a director, starring Sawera and Faisal in lead roles. That film flopped miserably and thus her wish of becoming a successful director remained unfulfilled.

Musarrat Shaheen and Masood Butt

One of the qualities of Musarrat Shaheen was that she was very skilled in setting up relationships between men and women. She played an important role in Sangeeta and Humayun Qureshi's wedding. She told Sangeeta that Humayun Qureshi loved her immensely. Sangeeta did not believe this, so Musarrat Shaheen took her to Humayun's house. When Sangeeta entered Humayun Qureshi's room, she saw that her pictures were displayed on the walls of the room. Seeing that scene, her heart became soft for Humayun Qureshi. Later, Sangeeta married Humayun Qureshi. You have already read those details in Sangeeta's story.

Similarly, Musarrat Shaheen played a prominent role in filmmaker Sohail Butt and Ishrat Chaudhary's love. The details are that Sohail Butt saw Ishrat Chaudhary at an event and fell in love with her. He talked to Musarrat Shaheen to introduce him to Ishrat.

Ishrat Chaudhry was a beautiful prostitute from the red-light district. She was very bold and daring when it came to sex and was also remembered as Sex Kitten. She had also married Shahid and claimed that Shahid would never leave her. But

Shahid could not stay in one place and was like a nomad, so he left Ishrat Chaudhary after a few years.

Musarrat Shaheen said to Sohail Butt, "Ishrat is an unsophisticated woman; you will not get anything from her. If you want to be friends, do it with me, I will fill your life with peace." But he was adamant that he would only be friends with Ishrat Chaudhry.

Musarrat Shaheen befriended both of them. Sohail Butt and Ishrat Chaudhry enjoyed the colors of life, but after some time they had a quarrel and became estranged to each other. But Musarrat Shaheen kept meeting with Sohail Butt.

When a friend asked Musarrat about Sohail Butt and her relationship with him, she replied that Sohail was like her son. But the readers should remember that even before that, Musarrat Shaheen used to call another person her son, the description of which is as follows. Read the story and judge for yourself.

Masood Butt

Masood Butt is a senior director of Pakistan film industry. He has presented many successful films to the public. The late Sultan Rahi also worked with him in notable films like "Dara Baloach," "Madam Rani," "Qaidi," "Majhu," "Bala Peer Da" and "Sakhi Badshah."

In his youth, Masood Butt also resorted to the services of Musarrat Shaheen. Since she was a dancer, she had good relations with all the girls in the dance world like Nazli, Muzla, Ishrat Chaudhary, Parveen Bobby, Najma, Rumani and Anita etc. The actress Anita was a beautiful dancer. Masood Butt fell in love with her. In those days, Masood Butt often came to Musarrat Shaheen's house, who used to call Masood Butt her son. He also used to call Musarrat his mother. Masood Butt told Musarrat Shaheen that he had fallen in love with Anita and asked her to introduce him to Anita. And so, Musarrat did this.

After a few meetings, both got married. But even after the marriage, Masood Butt kept going to Musarrat Shaheen's house. After the marriage, Anita gave birth to a daughter. After the birth of the daughter, Masood Butt started staying away from Anita. Often, Anita and Masood Butt would fight and their reconciliation would take place at Musarrat Shaheen's house.

One day, Sultana, the maid of Musarrat Shaheen, was cleaning the house when she suddenly entered her bedroom and saw that Masood Butt and Musarrat Shaheen were engaged in strange activities in the room. Shocked, she left the room and informed Anita about the whole situation. When Anita asked Masood Butt about it, there was a big fight between the two. Musarrat Shaheen took notice of the actions of her maid Sultana and engaged her male servants to hound Sultana. Sultana managed to get rid of those beastly people with great difficulty and she ran away to Anita. Thus, she stayed with Anita for some time. It should be remembered that Sultana belonged to Dera Ismail Khan, and Musarrat Shaheen brought her specially from Dera Ismail to Lahore for household tasks.

By reading the above story, you must have analyzed Musarrat Shaheen as a mother and Masood Butt as a son.

Starring Tariq Shah and Musarrat Shaheen

Tariq Shah is a senior actor of Pakistan film industry. Director Muhammad Akram's film "April Fool" was his debut film, which was released on 10 June 1977. He continued to play old characters in Urdu and Punjabi films, but he also played the role of a hero in Pashto films.

When Badar Munir, the hero of Pashto films, increased his compensation from 100,000 to 200,000, the filmmakers started casting Tariq Shah as the hero. Since the pairing of Musarrat Shaheen with Badar Munir was very popular, Musarrat Shaheen was cast with Tariq Shah. Along with being a couple in the films, Musarrat Shaheen and Tariq Shah decided to become a couple in real life as well. When they both fell in love, at that time they had entered their middle age and youth was far away from them.

Both were enjoying their love. If one had to look for Tariq Shah in the studio, he would first find out which film set Musarrat Shaheen's shooting was going on in, because at whichever set Musarrat Shaheen was shooting, Tariq Shah would also be standing there watching.

There is another story of that time that both of them were working on a film titled "Haseena Chakar Baaz" and were not separated even for a moment. They even used to jog together in the park of Model Town in the early morning. It was felt that there is one soul in two bodies.

They also transferred their love to their children. It so happened that Tariq Shah's son and Musarrat Shaheen's daughter played their childhood roles in a Pashto film "Nai Laila Naya Majnu." After being in love for some time, both of them parted ways because old age love cannot last for long.

Apart from Tariq Shah, Musarrat Shaheen also romanced a boy named Asif who worked as an office boy in the studio. Musarrat Shaheen had once said that she was truly in love with Asif but people thought it was a flirtation. During their love relationship, news of their marriage also appeared in newspapers. But social inequalities ended their love and they became strangers forever. Musarrat Shaheen also performed dance numbers during her peak. She performed in a grand wedding ceremony for Bashir Ahmed Balour, son of the former Federal Minister of Railways, in Peshawar. Musarrat made such angles of her body that men got uncontrollable and grabbed her. At that time, she was wearing a very short dress that was easy to remove from her body.

Musarrat Shaheen and Politics

In the general elections of 1997, Musarrat Shaheen formally announced her entry into politics. On this announcement, Musarrat Shaheen separated from the film industry and formed a political party in the name of Tehrik-e-Masawat. She participated in the election in her native of constituency Dera Ismail Khan. Musarrat Shaheen's opponents included famous religious scholar Maulana Fazal ur Rahman and cricketer Imran Khan. She made huge posters and banners that read "She is neither going to bow down nor sell out." Those who personally know Musarrat Shaheen are aware of how many times she had bowed down and sold out. During the election, she kept calling herself by the name of Tigress.

The big problem for Maulana Fazal ur Rahman was how to get rid of this 'obscene' woman. Maulana Fazal ur Rahman's supporters told him that M. Yusuf, the editor of the monthly magazine "Shama," had an album of Musarrat Shaheen's semi-nude photographs, and if requested, the album could be presented to him. But Fazal ur Rahman refused to do so.

Another supporter said that he could release Musarrat Shaheen's film "Gringo" within the constituency, in which she had stripped the film's villain of his male virtues with the help of sharp scissors and was enjoying watching the writhing lump of flesh herself. But Maulana Fazal ur Rahman said that he would not use any obscene tactic.

Musarrat Shaheen called Maulana "Maulana Diesel," but he considered silence a better response. After that, Musarrat Shaheen also said that seeing her, the clerics lost their minds. But despite all those tactics, she lost badly in the election. Today, she is neither a politician nor a film actor. Someone jokingly showed her the path to politics, which became her failure and not a success.

Nadira

NADIRA

From the Brothel to the Grave

Tall, with charming features, gazelle eyes, rosy lips, a beautiful smiling face, plump body, and immense feminine attraction, whoever saw her would be left staring and wondering how God decorated the world with beautiful faces.

Yes! I was admiring the actress Nadira. She was also worthy of praise for her beauty. Nadira was the only artist in the film industry with such a look and feel and had no equal.

Family Background

Nadira belonged to the red-light district of Lahore. Her real name was Farah and her filmic name was Nadira, which was given to her by director Younis Malik. Nadira's mother, Naseem alias Jiya, used to perform small roles in the films.

In those days, Naseem alias Jiya was the courtesan of filmmaker and director Ashraf Khan, who produced a film titled "Mangti" on 26 May 1961 and then announced he would produce another film called "Chaudah Saal." Naseem alias Jiya was also given a role in that film. A new hero, Sikandar, also acted in the movie "Chaudah Saal." Sikandar was very handsome. After seeing the beauty of Sikandar, Naseem threw the net of her coquetries on him and he fell in love with her.

Then Naseem simultaneously targeted Ashraf Khan and Sikandar for her false love. Naseem was the courtesan of Ashraf Khan for a monthly payment, and she used to receive money from him and indulged in sex with Sikandar. In that love game, she became pregnant and after some time gave birth to a baby girl named Farah. People thought that the baby girl belonged to Ashraf Khan because he gave Naseem a monthly compensation for living with him, but the girl looked like Sikandar. Wise people understood that something was wrong. In those days, Naseem left the brothel and came permanently to Ashraf's house.

It should be remembered that Ashraf Khan's film "Chaudah Saal" was released on April 19, 1968. When Ashraf Khan was fed up with Naseem alias Jiya, he left her. When Jiya found no other abode, she came back to the brothel. Jiya became so busy in the revelries of the brothel that her few years passed in peace but she was compelled by her heart. One day a rich man came to brothel and Jiya fell in love with him so much that after a few meetings she married him. She left the red-light district but before leaving she handed over her daughter Farah (Nadira) to her sister Sayyan and her aunt.

Farah was raised very well by Sayyan and her aunt. When Farah entered adulthood, her beauty started to be discussed everywhere. Her beauty became a money machine for Sayyan. That machine performed so well that Sayyan became very rich within a few years.

Farah's youthful exuberance fooled many. She built a beautiful bungalow for herself. Apart from that, her house was filled with three cars and lot of jewelry. Farah made the rounds in the Arab countries and collected enough Riyal. After Babra, she was the one who earned the most Riyals in one tour.

Arrival in Film World and Marriage

When actress Anjuman's films became successful, she started to misbehave with filmmakers and directors. The success of "Chan Varyam," "Sher Khan," "Sala Sahib," "Dhi Rani," "Qudrat," "Dou Begh Zameen," "Lawaris," "Choru Qutb," "Rustam Te Khan," "Dara Baloch," "Lal Tufan," "Sholay," "Baghi," "Baz Shahbaz," "Lagan" and "Qeemat" etc. made Anjuman very arrogant and she used to call herself a superstar. She would make the filmmakers visit her again and again regarding the dates of the film, due to which they became very upset. She also misbehaved with several filmmakers. Seeing the situation, director Younis Malik was also worried as the actress refused to perform in his film "Meri Adalat." So, Younis Malik announced in the studio that he would come up with a new heroine in competition with Anjuman.

Thus, he reached out to the red-light district in search of a new heroine. When he reached Sayyan's brothel, he was surprised to see the extremely beautiful girl. The eyes of that beautiful girl had a great impact on Younis Malik's heart. Seeing her, Younis Malik felt as if he had found his destination. That beautiful face belonged to the actress Nadira.

After a few meetings, Younis Malik cast Nadira in his film "Meri Adalat." The shooting of the film started and anyone who saw Nadira on the film set could not hold back from praising her.

Unfortunately, in those days, a very cunning and clever excise officer named Mubeen Malik used to come to Nadira's brothel. Nadira got tempted by his lies and became victim to his false love. One day, Nadira left Younis Malik's film incomplete and ran away with Mubeen Malik.

There was a hidden story behind Nadira's eloping. It so happened that when Nadira started earning in the red-light district, she used to give a regular share of the earnings to her aunt Sayyan and her paternal aunt. But they both demanded more money. Meanwhile, Nadira got the chance to perform in Younis Malik's film "Meri Adalat." Then they thought that Nadira's earnings would increase and hence, they started demanding more money, which often led to quarrels in the house. Nadira was very worried about the situation. One day, she got fed up and called Mubeen Malik to take her away from her home.

Mubeen Malik immediately came to Nadira, took her to his friend Ijaz Chaudhry's house and stayed there with her. One day, Mubeen Malik suddenly thought that Nadira's relatives might inform the police that their daughter had been kidnapped by him. So, he staged a marriage drama with the help of his friend Ijaz Chaudhry.

He wrote on a stamped piece of paper on Nadira's behalf that she had come of her own free will and wanted to marry Mubeen Malik. When the lawyer asked Nadira to sign the stamp paper, she asked what the matter was. The lawyer replied that because of the paper, her family cannot forcefully take her back and so, she signed the paper. Beneath that stamped paper was the marriage contract and Nadira also signed it in a state of worry after the stamped paper. In that way, she became the wife of Mubeen Malik.

Two days after it, a person from the Middle East called Nadira to his bungalow in Muslim Town. She went there and performed dance numbers for two days.

In the same way, she performed many dance numbers in various bungalows and earned millions. There was a time when she spent a whole month performing dance numbers and did not spare a single night for Mubeen Malik. That situation was intolerable for Mubeen Malik. During the same time, Nadira came to know about the marriage drama and she demanded a divorce from Mubeen Malik. He was already worried about Nadira's wrongdoings, so he immediately divorced her.

After the divorce, Nadira resettled in the brothel and her fortune blossomed upon her return to the brothel. It so happened that director Altaf Hussain cast her in his film "Nishan" and at the same time Younis Malik also gave her a chance to perform in his film "Akhri Jang."

Thus, Altaf Hussain's film "Nishan" was released on July 4, 1986 after its completion and became Nadira's debut film. Younis Malik's film "Akhri Jang" was released on 17 August 1986 and was a huge success across the country.

Anjuman and Nadira

Anjuman and Nadira were against each other from the beginning. One of the reasons was that Younis Malik was angry with Anjuman, thus introducing Nadira into films, which Anjuman was very sad about.

The second reason was Mubeen Malik, who first became the husband of Nadira and later of Anjuman. Both actresses would get angry upon seeing each other and expressed their anger by spitting in front of each other.

When a friend asked Nadira why she spat while looking at Anjuman, she said that she had spat on Mubeen Malik and Anjuman is now licking her spit. The reason given by Anjuman was that Mubeen Malik had spat on a vile woman like Nadira, meaning that she was not worthy to be called the wife of a man like Mubeen Malik.

Both of them had their own justifications, which would have made Mubeen Malik very happy.

Some Famous Films of Nadira

Title of Film	Director	Release Date
Nishan	Altaf Hussain	4-Jul-1986
Akhri Jang	Younis Malik	17-Aug-1986
Badal	Younis Malik	7-Aug-1987
Nachay Nagin	Haider Chaudhry	25-Sep-1987
Mafroor	Hassan Askari	18-May-1988
Miss Allah Rakhi	Haider Chaudhry	7-May-1989
Tees Maar Khan	Iqbal Kashmiri	10-Nov-1989
Mujrim	Haider Chaudhry	22-Dec-1989
Puttar Jaggay Da	Hassan Askari	8-Jun-1991
Watan Ke Rakhwalay	Husnain	23-Jun-1991
Nadira	Altaf Hussain	2-Aug-1991
Sher Afgan	Younis Malik	1-Nov-1991
Muhammad Khan	Altaf Hussain	10-Sep-1993
Laila	Nazar Islam	14-Oct-1994

List of Nadira's films shows that she worked with some of the best directors of her time namely Altaf Hussain, Younis Malik, Haider Chaudhary, Kaifi, Hassan Askari, Iqbal Kashmiri, and Nazar Islam. She acted in more than fifty films during her eight-year career. A film also named "Nadira" was made by director Altaf Hussain. Nadira did her work with dedication and love, she was not convinced to signing for more films but only believed in quality.

Haider Chaudhary's film "Nache Nagin" became a hit due to Nadira's excellent dances. Raza Mir's "Naag Mani," Iqbal Kashmiri's "Jadu" and Haider Chaudhry's "Jogi" had already been successful on the subject of snakes.

Nadira's Marriage to Ejaz Malik

Haji Ghulam Muhammad had a jewelry business in Lahore's Suha Bazar. His son, Ejaz Malik, was a handsome and virtuous young man who worked with his father in the jewelry shop. Mr. Haji had married Ejaz Malik at the beginning of his youth so that he would avoid bad habits. But still some of Ejaz's friends were very wicked. They often used to visit the red-light district and, on their return, they would tell Ejaz the stories of the fairies of the red-light district. Those boys had sexual relations with Madiha Shah, Labna Khattak and Sapna etc. Ejaz Malik forbade a close friend of his to go to Madiha Shah several times.

One day, that friend took Ejaz Malik to Nadira's brothel under the pretext of a visit to the red-light district. When Ejaz saw Nadira, he was left staring at her. He didn't know whether he should go home or stay at the brothel. Nadira was also happy seeing Ejaz, knowing that a new victim was eager to come into the trap. On that day, Ijaz reached his home with great difficulty.

He then realized what a woman is, and all his principles became blurred in front of the beauty of a woman. He thought that he had forbidden his friends for no reason and that he should have gone to Nadira long ago. All the things were playing in his mind like a movie. He was constantly berating himself and was busy trying to forget the passing moments of his life.

As Ejaz Malik was a rich man, spending money was a trivial thing for him. He decided to place the wealth at Nadira's feet. To convince Nadira economically, he also bought her three vehicles worth ten million and built a bungalow worth forty million in Model Town.

As Nadira was a beautiful prostitute, rich landlords and industrialists used to visit her brothel with millions of rupees. Even the sheikhs of the Arab countries generously gave financial support to her. An Arab sheikh also built Nadira a bungalow worth nine million in Model Town and in addition gave her millions of riyals in cash. Nadira gave great importance to that sheikh, in return for his favors, and she surrendered her brightening body to the lust of him several times. The audacity of the Arab Sheikh also made Nadira the mother of a beautiful baby girl.

Ejaz Malik was aware of Nadira's first child but still he was forced by his heart to marry her. Nadira kept the following two conditions for marriage:

1. Ejaz Malik would divorce his first wife.

2. He would raise Nadira's daughter from the sheikh as a father.

Ejaz Malik accepted the above conditions without any hesitation. After agreeing to the conditions, Nadira married Ejaz. He was very happy to marry Nadira and considered himself the luckiest man in the world. He kept the marriage a secret for some time but later made it public on the occasion of director Hasnain's film release, titled "Mehbooba." It should be noted that the film "Mehbooba" was released on November 6, 1992. After the marriage, Ejaz Malik forbade Nadira from acting in films. Earlier, he had also forbidden her from acting in films and due to this reason, Nadira could sign fewer films in her eight-year tenure.

Nadira's Murder

Nadira and Ejaz were living a great life together without any feelings of hardship. Nadira also gave birth to a cute son in those moments of happiness, whose birth was celebrated with great fanfare. Like Nadira, her son was also very beautiful. Suddenly, news came out that Nadira had been murdered.

Why and How Was Nadira Murdered?

On Sunday, 6 August 1995, Nadira was murdered by armed men near Gogo Restaurant. At that time, Nadira was going to have a meal in the car along with her husband and mother. The following are the suspected reasons for Nadira's murder.

Mahmood Alias Muda

1. Mahmood alias Muda (in charge of the red-light district) said that since Ejaz's family was very religious, his marriage to a prostitute was no less than a doomsday for his family.
2. Ejaz's father Haji Ghulam Muhammad also died due to the shock of his marriage.
3. Ejaz's mother was very traumatized so she stopped talking to him.
4. Ejaz's first wife was very upset about the marriage.

Since the whole family of Ejaz Malik was unhappy with his second marriage, they might have murdered Nadira.

Nadira's Aunt Sayyan (She Raised Nadira)

1. According to Sayyan, Ejaz and Nadira often used to fight over property and Ejaz had threatened to kill her several times.
2. Ejaz Malik had also sold two vehicles of Nadira's.
3. He had also taken 9 million rupees in the form of cash from Nadira.
4. He often asked Nadira for a share of her earnings so he could give it to his first wife and children, but Nadira refused.
5. Ejaz had also invested 15 million rupees of Nadira in his business.

6. Apart from that, Ejaz's business was also suffering from recession and thus, he was relying on Nadira's earnings.

Some people also believe that before marrying Nadira, Ejaz had sexual relations with Madiha Shah and she was very angry about his marriage with Nadira, so she thought that since Nadira had taken her friend away from her, she should kill her to avenge her friend's separation.

Naseem Alias Jiya

Nadira's mother Naseem gave a statement in favor of Ejaz. This shows that she also wanted to take some revenge upon Nadira. Since Naseem had left Nadira with Sayyan when she was young, Sayyan started receiving her share when Nadira got mature and started earning. Naseem did not get anything from Nadira's earnings and she did not even let her mother come close to her. For that reason, she was angry with Nadira.

The above statements show that Nadira might have been murdered by Ejaz Malik and his family because they were not happy with the marriage. After becoming a mother of two children, Nadira was no longer as attractive for Ejaz as before, so he began to ignore her. The first wife was also unhappy with Nadira. Nadira's mother also joined Ejaz in this murder and thus, they suppressed the case forever by paying a heavy bribe to the police.

Nadira's Funeral

A strange situation also occurred at Nadira's funeral. People from the film industry believed that Nadira was a film heroine, so her funeral procession should be taken out from her current residence, Tariq Block, Garden Town.

Mahmood alias Muda believed that since Nadira was a prostitute and was closely related to the red-light district, her funeral procession should be taken out from the Tabbi area.

Finally, Muda's suggestion was accepted and Nadira's funeral procession was taken out from the red-light district. Unhappy with that, film personalities did not attend Nadira's funeral.

Neeli.

NEELI

Beautiful Name With a Beautiful Performance

The name of beautiful lady with sharp features, inebriated eyes, an attractive figure, a long thin nose and a performance with beautiful coquetries is Neeli.

This slim and smart girl made the moviegoers crazy right from her debut movie. Her arrival was a huge test for the heavyweight heroines. Let's read the story of this fascinating beauty.

A beautiful baby girl was born in the red-light district of Hyderabad. Her parents named her Nilofar. A few years after her birth, Nilofar's mother handed her over to her sister Mukhtar Begum and eloped with a high-born man. Mukhtar Begum brought her up.

Nilofar spent her childhood days in the lap of the famous actress Chakori. She belongs to a very famous artist family and she is also the cousin of actress Anjuman. Therefore, the dance and music were hereditary for her. Apart from dance, Nilofar also received curriculum education. She did her matriculation in Hyderabad and F.A. in Lahore. As soon as she entered adulthood, like other artists, she travelled to Lahore and camped in the red-light district. When she could not find a suitable place to stay in the middle of the red-light district, she made a small house in front of the garbage heap as her abode, so as to stay near the red-light district. Seeing Nilofar's beauty and body flexibility, many high-born men, industrialists and landlords fell at her feet. In this way, Nilofar made a status for herself even while living in front of the pile of dirt.

Arrival in Films and Younis Malik

In those days, Anjuman was the ruling actress in Punjabi films and after success of many films, her popularity increased a lot. All filmmakers and directors were unhappy with Anjuman's behavior. During the shooting of a film, Anjuman and director Younis Malik had exchanged harsh words. Younis Malik announced that he would introduce a new heroine as a replacement of Anjuman.

To achieve this goal, Younis Malik turned to the red-light district and found Nilofer there. Seeing her appearance and performance, Younis Malik realized that he could end the monopoly of Anjuman. He changed Nilofar's name to Neeli. During the same time, Younis Malik met Farah and he changed Farah's name to Nadira. Thus, Younis Malik got two girls for the film at the same time. The presence of Neeli and

Nadira gave Younis Malik some peace of mind that he could succeed in making Anjuman a flop.

He started filming after casting Neeli in his film "Aakhri Jang." The film was released on August 17, 1986. Neeli's debut film became a super hit and the slim and smart heroine became the talk of the town. Neeli was given a warm welcome by the moviegoers as her arrival enabled them to get rid of the fat actresses like Anjuman.

Since the credit for finding Neeli went to Younis Malik, he often received physical compensation from her. One day, Younis Malik was expressing his love to Neeli as usual in the red-light district and Neeli was also eager to give her everything in response, when suddenly the Tabbi police caught both of them red-handed. The next morning, newspapers published their story.

After the film "Akhri Jang," director Sangeeta cast Neeli in her film "Qasam Munne Ki." That film was released on March 6, 1987. After that, "Choroun Ki Baraat," "Lava," "Baazi," "Sakhi Daata," "Maula Baksh," "Haseena 420," and "Madam Bawri" etc. made Neeli famous all over Pakistan.

After this fame, Neeli also got very arrogant like Anjuman. As Neeli was Anjuman's cousin, they were of the same blood, which always provoked Neeli into disloyalty.

It so happened that there was one day of work left for Younis Malik's film Yaraana but Neeli refused to shoot anymore. Younis Malik tried to convince her that she should not do that, as it would cause him a big loss. But Neeli did not listen to Younis Malik and went away in a fit of temper. Likewise, Younis Malik had to suffer a loss of 50,000 Rupees as Neeli left the shooting incomplete.

Neeli as an Actress

After Babra Sharif, Neeli was the only actress who played all kinds of roles in films and her every role was loved by the public. Neeli performed with Sultan Rahi, Javed Sheikh, Ismail Shah, Izhar Qazi and Ghulam Mohiuddin. She also played the roles of Household, Modern and Sexy Girl in films.

She played a very sexy role in filmmaker Sajjad Gul's film "Jou Dar Gaya Wah Mar Gaya" and became the talk of Pakistan. After that, Neeli played extremely obscene roles in "Harjai" and "Fareb." As Neeli was growing older, her inclination towards sexier roles was also increasing. Neeli is almost out of films these days.

Javed Shaikh – From Early Life to Neeli

Javed Sheikh belongs to Karachi; he completed his education in Karachi and also started his artistic journey from Karachi Television. Initially, he also performed in a few TV commercials, but when fortune favored him, he got a role in a film titled "Dhamaka" in 1974. Directed by Qamar Zaidi, the film flopped badly. Shabnam was the heroine with Javed Sheikh in that film. When Javed Shaikh's film debut failed, he moved to TV and gained national fame by playing the role of

Mansoor in the drama serial "Shama," written by Fatima Surraya Bajya.

Javed Sheikh's nature was very romantic from the beginning, due to which he is also called a ladykiller. Most of the girls seemed to be trapped in the vortex of his personality. Let us mention the girls trapped in the clutches of Javed Sheikh who had been in love with Javed Sheikh before Neeli.

Caroline

Caroline came from France and worked with Javed Sheikh in a TV commercial. Whenever Javed got the chance, he would trick Caroline with false promises. When she became trapped in his clutches, Javed Sheikh created a drama of love with Caroline and their love story became famous everywhere. But when Javed Sheikh got tired of Caroline, he started staying away from her. When Caroline saw his behavior, she was so heartbroken that she stopped trusting Pakistani men. In the face of this betrayal, she went back to France.

Shamsi Sheikh

Shamsi Sheikh was the second victim of Javed Sheikh. She was an aspiring model, but fate put her in the lap of Javed Sheikh. It should be remembered that Shamsi Sheikh played the memorable role of Nadia in director Shamim Aara's film "Playboy," which was released on September 5, 1978. The film became a super hit and won many awards.

Javed Sheikh, with his cleverness, convinced Shamsi to become his wife. They got married at the Metropole Hotel in Karachi. Shamsi accepted Javed as her everything and showered her all on him, but despite Javed's closeness, she could not understand him. Once when he went to France on a business trip, he sent divorce papers to Shamsi Sheikh. She lost her senses after seeing the divorce papers, but nothing could be done now.

Even after reaching France, Javed Sheikh did not stop flirting. There he became close to a foreign lady but she was very smart and well aware of the psychology of Pakistani men, and that they try to get the support of foreign ladies in order to live abroad and when going back, they do not even ask, "Are you okay?" Javed Sheikh got rid of that lady with great difficulty, left his business tour unfinished and returned to Pakistan. Upon return, he did not meet anyone for several days because the signs of embarrassment were evident on his face.

Zeenat Manghi

She belonged to a Sindhi family and was a very sensible and smart girl. She started her career by modeling on PTV and got a lot of fame from the advertisement of Rixona soap. When Javed Sheikh met Zeenat, he forgot all his old lovers after seeing her. Gradually, their series of meetings got longer. One day, Javed decided that he must marry Zeenat one way or another. After a few more meetings, he proposed and asked Zeenat to marry him.

Zeenat's family strongly opposed the marriage, but at that time she was overwhelmed with love and could not think of parting with Javed in any way. When Zeenat did not relinquish Javed Sheikh's love, her parents severed all ties with her. She did not care about her parents' separation and eventually married Javed Sheikh.

After his marriage to Zeenat, the doors of Javed Sheikh's fortune opened and he started getting projects on PTV as well as stage plays. He got a good role in Haseena Moin's famous drama "Ankahi" but left it unfinished and went abroad and thus got banned by PTV.

As fate was kind to him, PTV's ban proved to be temporary. In those days, the stars of Zeenat were having a positive impact on Javed Sheikh. Filmmaker and director Nazar Shabab launched the film "Kabhi Alviada Na Kehna" in Lahore. The story of the film was written by Ali Sufian Afaqi. Shabnam was the heroine of the film, while no suitable hero could be found. Satish Chand, a film distributor from Karachi, convinced Nazar Shabab to cast Javed Shaikh as the hero in the film. In that way, Javed Sheikh got a chance to come back to films after 9 years.

Most of the film was shot in Sri Lanka. When Javed Sheikh arrived in Sri Lanka for shooting, the first good news he got from Pakistan was that he had become a father of a child, which he was very happy about because Zeenat had revolutionized his life. He thought that if only Zeenat could have entered his life earlier, he would have had all the comforts of the world.

Sabeetha

Apart from Shabnam, another lady named Sabeetha was playing role in the film "Kabhi Alvida Na Kehna" and came from Sri Lanka. Seeing her beauty, Javed Sheikh fell in love with her. Whenever he was done shooting for the film, he would secure himself in her arms. Since Sabeetha herself was a free-spirited girl, she was openly wooing Javed Sheikh.

In Pakistan, Zeenat Manghi was rejoicing that Allah had blessed her with a beautiful son and her husband had become a film star. But she was not aware of Javed Sheikh's activities in Sri Lanka. After the shooting of the film was completed, Javed came to Pakistan, leaving her fresh love unfulfilled.

The film "Kabhi Alvida Na Kehna" was released on 18th September 1983 and did a lot of business all over Pakistan. Due to the success of the film, Javed Sheikh secured his place in the film industry. He told his friends that his success was due to his wife and child.

Javed left Karachi and moved to Lahore and took a rented bungalow there. The reputation of that bungalow was not good because after their marriage, Shahid and Babra Sharif had stayed also stayed in the same bungalow and after some time they got separated. People were scared for Javed and

Zeenat but they said, "We do not believe in superstition. As our love is true, we will never be separated."

A few months after coming to Lahore, a baby girl was born to Javed Sheikh. Thus, the presence of son and daughter completed their family.

After reaching Lahore, Javed Sheikh performed the roles in the following films:

Title of Film	Director	Release Date
Shadi Magar Adhi	Zafar Shabab	30-Mar-1984
Miss Colombo	Shamim Aara	30-Jun-1984
Bobby	Nazar Shabab	7-Sep-1984
Karaye Ke Goreelay	Waheeda Khan	16-Sep-1984
Tere Ghar ke Samnay	Zafar Shabab	14-Dec-1984
Hong Kong Ke Shoulay	Jaan Muhammad	30-Jun-1985
Jeene Nahi Dungi	Sangeeta	26-Jul-1985
Nadia	Nazar Shabab	4-Oct-1985
Mehndi	Altaf Hussain	1-Nov-1985

Salma Agha

Salma Agha has a big family. The name of her elderly lady was Naziran and she was a famous prostitute of Amritsar. People of that era were not so rich. The salary of a government employee was also fixed at 5 or 10 Rupees per month. But, to visit Naziran's brothel, one had to have at least 100 Rupees in pocket.

After Naziran, she was succeeded by her daughter Anwari who had such a magical voice that people would forget their way home. Anwari's daughter was Zarina, who was very beautiful. She also performed in a few films with the name of Nasreen. After that, she got married to a rich man named Agha Liaqat Gul. Zarina had two daughters and a son named Salma Agha, Satya Agha and Salman Agha respectively. This is how this family linage came into being: Naziran … Anwari … Zarina and Salma Agha

Salma Agha grew up in London and received her singing and dancing training from her maternal grandmother, Anwari. She was married to a Pakistani young man at the age of 16. Since she was not yet ready to become a mother and was fond of acting in films, she got divorce after a year.

Salma was then married to a businessman named Azhar. Her parents wanted to keep him as matrilocal, but he did not do so. Apart from this, Salma Agha was always busy dancing and singing and partying till late at night. She did not give time to her husband, due to which he became mentally ill and finally got depressed and divorced Salma Agha. After getting divorced, Salma Agha decided to work in films. She performed in B.R. Chopra's film "Nikah" which got a lot of fame.

There was a rich man named Mahmood Supra who knew the art of flirting with ladies. When Salma Agha went to London from Bombay, she met Mahmood Supra there. After few meetings, Salma and Mahmood became very close to each other. In those days, Salma Agha's mother fell ill and was admitted to a hospital in London. Mahmood Supra served Salma's mother Zarina a lot. On his insistence, Zarina engaged Salma and Mahmood Supra in the hospital. After the engagement, both of them started dating openly. Mahmood Supra spent many beautiful nights of his life in the embrace of Salma Agha.

After some time, Salma came to Pakistan. Javed Sheikh and Salma met for the first time during the event of Nazar Shabab's film "Rubi." The songs of that film were sung by Salma Agha. They met a second time during the shooting of the movie "Hum Aur Tum." Because director Hasan Askari had cast Javed Shaikh and Salma in that film, both of them tested each other during the filming.

On one hand, Salma was getting closer to Javed Sheikh; on the other hand, Mahmood was forcing Salma to marry. Salma imposed a condition on Mahmood Supra that he should first divorce his first wife and then she would marry him. Mahmood Supra refused to accept any of Salma's conditions. Eventually, Salma parted ways with Mahmood Supra.

After separating from Mahmood Supra, she lured Javed Sheikh into her trap by showing him dreams of a golden future. Javed Sheikh came to Salma's words and married her.

After marrying Salma Agha, Javed Sheikh separated from his ex-wife Zeenat Manghi and also left his two children with her. Javed and Salma had been happily married for a short time but they began to ignore each other. Salma used to insult Javed everywhere and often spoke to him in a humiliating tone. Javed would not say anything and kept looking at her face because he was under her pressure. Salma wanted to take Javed with her to India but he was insisting to stay in Pakistan. Finally, their bond ended forever in mid 1988. It should be remembered that their relationship started during the film "Hum Aur Tum," which was released on 13 December 1985.

Salma Agha worked in Pakistani movies like "'Sherni," "Aik Se Barh kar Aik," "Bhabhi Diyan Choriyan," "Daag," "Taqat Ka Tufan," "Akhri Shikar," "Cobra" and "Bazar-e-Husn." After Javed Sheikh, Salma married squash coach Rehmat Khan. A boy and a girl were born to Salma from that marriage. Some time later Salma also got separated from Rehmat. She then befriended Faisal Tarar, the nephew of a police officer who was half Salma's age.

A few days ago, when she came to Multan to perform in a stage play "Aik Baar Milo Hum Se," she asked the drama producer to book single room for both of them. The producer booked room number 218 of the Holiday Inn for both of them. It was only two days after the drama started that Salma left the drama unfinished and went to Lahore, due to which the producer had to bear a big loss. It should be remembered that Salma had made a deal of 300,000 with the producer to perform in that drama. When Faisal's parents found out that their son had befriended Salma, they forbade him to meet her. Moreover, Faisal's maternal grandmother had taunted Salma a lot. When Salma realized that now Faisal would move away from her, she immediately started looking for a new victim. The goddess of fortune was kind to Salma and she befriended Aamir Khan, the director of a mobile company.

Javed Sheikh and Neeli

Javed Sheikh and Neeli first teamed up in director Jaan Muhammad's film, "Roop Ki Rani," which was released on 7 May 1989. At that time, Javed was trying to bear the pain of separation from Salma Agha. On the other hand, a few films of Neeli had flopped and she also had a quarrel with her benefactor, director Younis Malik.

The film "Roop Ki Rani" flopped badly. On the same day, May 7, 1989, the second film of Javed Sheikh and Neeli, titled "Madam Bawri," directed by Nazar Islam, was released. The film was a success but the hopes that Neeli had from the film could not be fulfilled, due to which she kept crying in her bedroom for many days.

Javed Sheikh and Neeli came close to each other while crying about the irony of the situation, so they decided that now they would conquer the film world. For said purpose, both of them started begging filmmakers for each other's casting. Both of them would sit and unburden their hearts for hours and take refuge in the bedroom to find peace. Both of them used to go to the studio in the same car.

One day when Neeli and Javed Sheikh got out of the car, it seemed that Neeli had just washed her hair, as fresh drops of water glistened in her disheveled hair. People in the studio thought that maybe they were married, but it was nothing like that, it was a form of love. Similarly, once both were staying in a five-star hotel in Karachi and both had booked a single room to stay in. When a journalist came to their room for an interview, Neeli and Javed Sheikh were sitting on the same bed talking about secrets. After saying hello to the journalist, Neeli went to the bathroom. The journalist saw that one of Neeli's earrings was lying on Javed Sheikh's bed. After a while, Neeli called Javed Sheikh from the bathroom and asked for her earring. When Neeli came out of the bathroom, the journalist pointed to her earring and asked, "Miss Neeli! What is this matter?" Neeli replied, "Everything works in the business of love. We did not book a single room to play tipcat, you are sensible, this is not a strange thing."

In October 1992, Neeli's secretary and hairdresser Zahoor alias Madhu Bala revealed that Neeli was very much in love with Javed Sheikh and that she had forgotten everything to be in love with him. She only wanted Javed to be the center of her attention and she had gone crazy and was blindly in love with him. He added that some people say that Javed Sheikh would give pocket money to Neeli, which Neeli needed. She worked in the films under the directio is completely wrong and there was no such thing. Javed Sheikh is a miser, so in fact Neeli spent on him. He said that he even did not know what spell Javed Sheikh had cast on Neeli; if he fought Neeli, she still fell into his embrace like a ripe fruit.

In September 1994, Javed Sheikh and Neeli had a falling out. Both of them were at odds with each other. The incident came to light when they returned from Turkey to Pakistan after completing the shooting of Syed Noor's film "Jeeva." After that, they did not attend the opening ceremony of filmmaker Sajjad Gul's film "Jou Dar Gaya Woh Mar Gaya" together. Apart from that, their attitude was not right during the filmmaking of "Mushkil," directed by Javed Sheikh – rather, Neeli used to go home quickly after dubbing her dialogues and nothing was discussed between the two. Neeli started coming to the studio with her aunt Mukhtar Begum instead of Javed Sheikh. At last sensible people understood that there was some problem between the two.

They reconciled in December 1994, but after some time they again became angry with each other. On investigation, it was found that Javed Sheikh was very angry with Neeli for her non-film activities. Neeli was in contact with many people without telling Javed Sheikh. Although Javed Sheikh is a very broad-minded person, he is not so open that he wanted people to consider his beloved as their personal property.

On the other hand, Neeli had spread the word among her sympathizers that Javed Sheikh had spent all her earnings and he had left her and was in love with the actress Meera. Long story short, the famous dress designer B.G. reconciled the two so that the couple could fall in love again.

Famous Films of Neeli

Title of Film	Director	Release Date	Result
Roop ki Raani	Jaan Muhammad	7-May-89	Golden Jubilee
Madam Bawri	Nazar Islam	7-May-89	Golden Jubilee
Ameer Khan	Younis Malik	6-Oct-89	Golden Jubilee
International Gureelay	Jaan Muhammad	27-Apr-90	Golden Jubilee
Jangju Gureelay	Aziz Tabassum	27-Apr-90	Golden Jubilee
Kaley Chour	Nazar Islam	4-Jan-91	Diamond Jubilee
Bakhtawar	Iqbal Kashmiri	1-Nov-91	Golden Jubilee
Khuda Gawah	Masood Butt	25-Mar-93	Silver Jubilee
Akhri Mujra	Shamim Aara	11-Nov-94	Average
Jeeva	Syed Noor	3-Mar-95	Golden Jubilee
Mushkil	Javed Sheikh	31-Mar-95	Average
Jou Dar Gaya Woh Mar Gaya	Iqbal Kashmiri	22-Sep-95	Golden Jubilee
Chief Sahib	Javed Sheikh	26-Mar-96	Platinum Jubilee

Neeli and Masood Butt

The director Masood Butt has been mentioned in the previous pages as well. He also had relationships with actresses Anita and Musarrat Shaheen. Neeli worked with Masood Butt in a few films and developed a close relationship with him, which Neeli needed at that time. She worked in the films under the direction of Masood Butt like "Hasina 420," "Khuda Gawah" and "Fareb."

In September 1996, the shooting of the film "Fareb" was taking place in Dr. Ehsan's bungalow. Sagheer Rana was the make-up man of the film who had some urgent work, due to which he sent another senior makeup man named Sadiq with the unit. When there was a break during the shooting, the members of the unit sat around and engaged in conversation. Neeli and Masood Butt also sat together in a room. After a short while, make-up man Sadiq went to the same room where Neeli and Masood Butt were sitting and talking about secrets. Sadiq saw that Masood Butt was holding Neeli's hand in his hand and was kissing her hand. Seeing Sadiq suddenly entering the room, Neeli got nervous. She asked Sadiq who he was and what he had come to the room to get. Sadiq said that he was the makeup man. Neeli started speaking loudly after hearing this. Meanwhile, all the members of the unit gathered there. Neeli accused Sadiq of staring at her and therefore she insulted him. Later, some respected people reconciled the two, but Neeli's actions came to light. It should be remembered that Masood Butt's film "Fareb" was released on October 10, 1997. Neeli's bold dances were also included in the film.

Neeli and Sarfraz Merchant

Sarfraz Merchant was very good at flirting with beautiful girls. He used to get a young girl under his influence in a moment; he was also very good at giving rein to the uncourteous and unruly girls. A young girl's soft body was his weakness and he found comfort in spending nights with young girls.

It was during those days when Sarfraz Merchant was staying at the Pearl Continental Hotel, Karachi, in April 1994. He told his friend Raheel that he was in the mood to spend the night with a girl and so a new girl should be called for him. Raheel obeyed Sarfraz Merchant and took Neeli to Sarfraz's room, number 335, on the night of 4 April 1994. Neeli showed Sarfraz Merchant her beautiful body that night, and made him forget the way home. That night, Sarfraz fell in love with Neeli.

Sarfraz Merchant was a businessman who was running Decora Furniture House in Karachi. He had no shortage of wealth and was married before meeting Neeli, who was deeply in love with Javed Sheikh in those days. She used to present her body comfortably in front of different people to pay for Javed Sheikh's expenses. A relationship with Sarfraz Merchant was also a link in that chain.

After the meeting on 14 April 1994, Sarfraz Merchant and Neeli met many times, the details of which are as follows.

1. They met several times in hotels at Karachi and Lahore.
2. Neeli used to talk to Sarfraz Merchant on his mobile number 225999 for several hours.
3. One day, both of them were staying at the Avari Hotel, Lahore. They hired a car from the hotel owners and reached Data Durbar, where Neeli took the hand of Sarfraz Merchant and swore to marry him.
4. When Neeli went to Manila for the shooting of "Jou Dar Gaya Woh Mar Gaya," Sarfaraz also reached there on 24 Dec 1994. There, both of them stayed in Shangrila Hotel. They came to Lahore after returning

from Manila and took temporary residence in a bungalow located in Gulberg.

5. A few days later, they both went to Holland again where they stayed in room 136 of the Crown Plaza Hotel.

6. After some time, both of them got married. A child was also born to them after the marriage. As mentioned in the previous pages, Neeli used to establish physical relations with various people for Javed Sheikh so that his expenses could be met.

According to the plan, Neeli demanded ten million Rupees from Sarfraz Merchant. She told Sarfaraz Merchant that she was making a film called "Chief Sahib" with Javed Sheikh and would return all the money to him after the release of the film.

On Neeli's insistence, Sarfraz Merchant gave her ten million Rupees. Javed Sheikh, with that money, made the film "Chief Sahib," which was released on March 26, 1996. The film did a lot of business but Sarfraz Merchant did not get anything and Javed Sheikh squandered all the money, while Sarfraz Merchant remained penniless. Sarfraz also divorced his first wife because of Neeli's apparent beauty and artificial love, but she did not give up her infidelity.

Apart from Sarfraz Merchant, Neeli also had relations with Karachi's Seth Anis, Jam Haider and Aziz Memon. Neeli used to do the dance numbers too. Sarfraz Merchant still has the video of dance number at Riyaz Churiwala's house in Lahore.

Let Me live – Mian Farzand Ali

Javed Sheikh's first film as a director was "Mushkil," which was released on March 31, 1995. The film did not do much business, but Javed Sheikh was definitely encouraged.

Meera was introduced in Javed Sheikh's second film "Chief Sahib." Meera had earlier worked on director Aman Mirza's film "Kanta," which was released on December 29, 1995. Mian Farzand Ali was known as a generous filmmaker in the film industry. Javed Sheikh did not let that great person live peacefully and finally he died in September 2000 as he was unable to bear the mental injuries given by Javed Sheikh. He kept telling Javed Shaikh "Let me live" until the last moment.

A few days ago, it was reported that after Sarfraz Merchant, Neeli got married to the owner of an airline company.

Mumtaz

MUMTAZ

Chadd Meri Beeni Na Maror

After Multan and Lahore, Gujrat also has the honor of unearthing many beauties, who belonged there, entering film world and making their name in the industry on the basis of their artistic abilities. Among those film heroines who came from Gujrat, Sabiha Khanum, Tassawar Khanum, Nisho and Mumtaz, etc. are worthy of a mention.

Suraiya, Mumtaz's mother, along with her six sisters came from the village of Gujrat, Lakhanwal, to Lahore's the red-light district. Suraiya's sisters began prostituting in the market. Besides Suraiya, Mehboob Mai, Musarrat Mai, and Manzoor Mai gained a lot of fame in the red-light district. The director Rasheed Akhtar used to appear often at Mehboob alias Bobby's brothel as well. But Suraiya's sisters could not run their business persistently in the brothel. A few of them eloped with their lovers. It was only Suraiya who displayed perseverance. She did not leave the brothel but stayed there and gave birth to children by different men. She gave birth to six sons and a daughter named Rifat.

In 1954, Rifat (Mumtaz) was born in a small room of an apartment in the red-light district. Suraiya was gratified at Mumtaz's birth but felt dejected that only one daughter was born, if three to four girls were born to her, then her retirement would have been spent in comfort and placidity. Whenever in the red-light district, a third or fourth daughter was born to some other prostitute, Suraiya would feel agonized. Mumtaz did not look very enchanting during her childhood and that was the reason that made Suraiya cry over her destiny.

Mumtaz's father was a well-off person who go caught into the trap of Suraya's coquetries at a tender age. Suraiya swindled him with her prostitute-like charms in such a way that he became bankrupt in the course of a few years. He could not even return to his family in such a state. He forcibly started selling roasted chickpeas in front of Suraiya's brothel, so she could realize that she had made a man go bankrupt. But she paid no heed to it.

Mumtaz gained her initial education from Asfiya New Model Girls High School. After that, she withdrew from her studies. When Mumtaz became a movie heroine, a journalist asked her about her education to which she replied that she could count currency notes.

During her childhood, Mumtaz often used to go to her father's cart to eat roasted chickpeas for free. One day, Suraiya caught sight of this incident and she became infuriated. She forbade Mumtaz forcefully from taking anything to eat from that man ever again. After this incident, Mumtaz stopped going there.

Mumtaz's Deflowering

As soon as Mumtaz stepped into her puberty, Suraiya became anxious about her deflowering. Suraiya contacted a few of her friends in Lahore, but no deal could be locked up.

Suraiya took Mumtaz along with her to Karachi and there she gathered a plenitude of money by entrapping a man. Later, she brought Mumtaz along with her to Lahore as Mumtaz's deflowering in Karachi was kept a secret. That was why, no one in the red-light district could be aware of it.

A few months later, Suraiya pretended Mumtaz was a virgin in front of a foreigner and received huge sums of money. Often, Suraiya used to feel delighted by mentioning the incidents of her shrewdness to people in the studio. This way, Mumtaz became an actress who was deflowered twice.

Love Affair with Sarwar

As Mumtaz was Suraiya's only child, that is why she was her darling. She often used to follow her heart; her mother was helpless before her every desire. Naila Cinema was close to the red-light district in Lahore and beside it, there was a gymnasium for wrestlers where heavy-built wrestlers used to learn methods of wrestling. Whenever Mumtaz wished, she used to leave her house and head towards Naila Cinema or stand in front of the gymnasium to see the wrestlers.

Mumtaz had been fond of watching films since her childhood. She was a fan of Nadeem (an actor). Whenever any of

Nadeem's films were released in Naila Cinema, she used to rush to it immediately. If she ran out of money, she used to contact the manager of Naila Cinema and sit in the cinema hall.

Sarwar used to feel overjoyed at his heart by seeing the sprouting youth of Mumtaz and made plans about entrapping her. He often used to say to Mumtaz that she could come to watch a film whenever she wished to. On the other hand, Mumtaz was a flirt too. She accepted this offer without any refusal. This way, Sarwar's arrow hit the right spot and Mumtaz became Sarwar's reserve.

Sarwar's age-old wish was fulfilled. Mumtaz started to look for excuses to meet Sarwar, and this way their relationship became firm. When the lights in Naila Cinema used to become lusterless, bells started to ring in their hearts and they used to overflow in their fondness to such a degree that their return home became hard. This love progression continued for many months, but then in the course of their life, they became separated.

Peshawari Friend

Mumtaz was climbing gradually the ladder of popularity in the red-light district. Besides Lahore, people from remote areas used to come to watch Mumtaz's dance performances. Mumtaz's mother used to collect money with a display of great mannerisms during the dance performance.

A fine-looking boy from Peshawar also used to appear at Mumtaz's brothel. As he was a Pashtun, his fair complexion looked good to Mumtaz's eyes. Mumtaz used to become free of her clients in haste and then entertain him exclusively in seclusion. He also used to travel from Peshawar to Lahore only for the sake of Mumtaz.

Similarly, there was a paper merchant, who was Mumtaz's lover as well, and he used to put all his earnings at the feet of Mumtaz's mother so that she would assign one of Mumtaz's nights to him. Mumtaz's mother was a dexterous lady: on those nights when Mumtaz was unavailable, Suraiya herself used to amuse him.

Tour to United Arab Emirates

Just like Babra Sharif and Aliya, Mumtaz also resorted to Arab Sheikhs to fill her pockets. The actress Cham Cham's brother Jaja used to take girls from the red-light district abroad, after deciding on his commission. In this regard, Mumtaz contacted Jaja so that an arrangement could be made for her to go abroad as well, and that she would pay Cham Cham and Jaja's commission. Cham Cham recommended Mumtaz to Jaja.

In those days, Sultan An-Nayhan's nearest beloved, Sultan Hamdan, was a voluptuary of Pakistani girls. Jaja decided all matters for Mumtaz and sent her to Sultan Hamdan in the United Arab Emirates. Mumtaz gave the Sheikh plenty of corporeal services. The Sheikh praised Marhaba for every charm of Mumtaz. Mumtaz also shot all the arrows of her bow at the Sheikh. The sultan was pleased with her and showered her with a lot of gifts. Apart from that, he also gifted her many precious diamonds. When Mumtaz returned to her homeland after the tour, she gave no share of diamonds to Cham Cham and Jaja. This became a bone of contention between both of them. This incident became renowned in the whole red-light district – that Mumtaz had grabbed all the money alone by befooling Cham Cham.

Mumtaz and Sheikh Mushtaq

Sheikh Mushtaq used to do business in Lahore. Besides that, being a filmmaker, he produced four films. The filmmaker Sheikh Mushtaq introduced director Altaf Hussain for the first time in his film "Panchi Te Pardesi." This film was released on 27 February 1969. In addition to that, Sheikh Mushtaq got Altaf Hussain to direct "Veer Pyare" and "Do Nain Sawali" as well. As Sheikh Mushtaq had abundant wealth, he considered it his right to play with the girls of the market. He used to visit Suraiya's brothel from time to time, but when Mumtaz grew up, then he became a habitual visitor. In those days, Mumtaz had not been introduced to films yet. Sheikh Mushtaq derived great pleasure from Mumtaz's beauty. In exchange for that, Suraiya also received the price she demanded. As long as Sheikh Mushtaq remained encaptivated by Mumtaz's tresses, he kept Mumtaz away from films. But when Sheikh Sahib became tired of her, Suraiya decided to get Mumtaz into films.

Entrance to Films and Ilyas Kashmiri

To bring Mumtaz into films, Suraiya had already contacted influential individuals. In this regard, Suraiya made Mumtaz available to many people even for free. Suraiya's efforts proved to be fruitful and the director Nazar-ul-Islam gave Mumtaz the role of a dancer in his film "Ehsas." Take note that "Ehsas" was released on 22 December 1972. Additionally, Suraiya had also entrapped a famous actor, Ilyas Kashmiri. He used to pay Mumtaz monthly so that she could serve him exclusively.

One day, Suraiya discussed Mumtaz with Ilyas Kashmiri. Ilyas Kashmiri said that he was arranging Mumtaz's physical tests at the time, as soon as she cleared the test, he would bring her into films. This way Ilyas Kashmiri spent a number of months with her. When he got tired of her, he discussed Mumtaz with a filmmaker, Chaudhry Ajmal. In those days, Chaudhry Ajmal was making a film, "Ziddi," in which Yusuf Khan, Ejaz, Firdous and Zamurd were acting. On Ilyas Kashmiri's persuasive recommendation, Chaudhry Iqbal provided Mumtaz with an opportunity to be a dancer in his film. Iqbal Kashmiri was the director of "Ziddi," whereas Master Abdullah was its music composer. The words of the song which were penned for Mumtaz, go this way:

> *Leave me! Do not twist my wrist!*
> *And do not break the glass bangles*

When this film was released on 16 January 1973, this song rocked the whole of Pakistan. As the song became a hit,

Mumtaz became a hit too. This way, Mumtaz earned fame with just one song.

After that, Mumtaz got work in the director Iqbal Kashmiri's film "Banarsi Thug," owing to Ilyas Kashmiri. In "Banarsi Thug," Ilyas Kashmiri and Munawar Zareef were playing the main roles. Mumtaz filmed a glamorous song in this film as well:

> *I fell in love with great difficulty*
> *Seldom are such chances available*

This way, Mumtaz gained fame in film in exchange for glamorizing Ilyas Kashmiri's nights. Witnessing Mumtaz's fame, the filmmaker Chaudhry Ajmal started drooling over her. He was after Ilyas Kashmiri to let him get closer to Mumtaz. Ilyas Kashmiri and Chaudhry Ajmal were close friends, which is why, keeping in view this relationship, Ilyas Kashmiri gifted Mumtaz to Chaudhry Ajmal. Ajmal kept Mumtaz as a mistress for some time. Later on, Mumtaz got married as per convention.

Mumtaz's Inartistic Voice

In terms of voice, Mumtaz was miserable. She had a clattering voice. It seemed as if she had a sore throat and she was not taking any medicine to treat that. She had the capacity to ruin the best scripts. People seated in the cinema hall also used to show aversion upon listening to her voice.

A famous journalist, Sufyan Afaqi, wrote director S. Suleman's film "Intezar." He had gone abroad for some work-related tasks. When he returned, S. Salman had already started shooting the film after completing its cast. Mumtaz, in that film, was playing the role of a modern girl who received her education in London. On one hand, Mumtaz was unschooled, while on the other, her voice seemed weird while speaking English. When Mr. Afaqi observed this situation, he could not keep himself from lamenting over it.

Mumtaz had maltreated some of the best dialogues. But thanks be to God, the film was still a success. During Mumtaz's whole career, her voice remained problematic persistently, which led plenty of filmmakers and directors to bear huge losses.

Mumtaz's Film Career

Mumtaz had initiated her career as a dancer. Later on, she was cast as a heroine. She worked with commendable directors of the film industry including S. Suleman, Iqbal Kashmiri, Waheed Dar, Nazar ul Islam, Haider Chaudhry, M. Akram, and Altaf Hussain, etc.

At the beginning of her career, Mumtaz was thin and had a well-shaped body. But later on, she started gaining weight and the nature of her character altered as well. In "Sala Sahib," "Dhi Rani," "Shan," "Murad Khan," "Gangwa," etc., her stoutness could be seen distinctively. Let's examine a list of some of Mumtaz's films.

Title of film	Director	Release Date	Outcome
Ehsas	Nazar ul Islam	22-Dec-1972	Successful
Ziddi	Iqbal Kashmiri	16-Jan-1973	Successful
Banarsi Thug	Iqbal Kashmiri	20-Oct-1973	Successful
Intezar	S. Suleman	9-Aug-1974	Successful
Naukar Vohti Da	Haider Chaudhry	26-Jul-1974	Successful
Shikar	S. A. Hafiz	23-Aug-1974	Average
Jadu	Iqbal Kashmiri	13-Dec-1974	Successful
Pyar Ka Mausam	Munawar Rasheed	4-Apr-1975	Successful
Shareef Badmash	Iqbal Kashmiri	11-Jul-1975	Successful
Talash	Pervaiz Malik	22-Jan-1976	Successful
Ann Daata	Iqbal Yusuf	26-Sep-1976	Successful
Amber	Nazar ul Islam	6-Jan-1978	Successful
Dubai Chalo	Haider Chaudhry	3-Nov-1979	Successful
Sala Sahib	Altaf Hussain	2-Aug-1981	Successful
Dou Baigh Zameen	Younis Malik	19-Mar-1982	Successful
Naukar Te Maalik	Hasnain	2-Apr-1982	Successful
Dhi Rani	Altaf Hussain	19-Apr-1985	Successful
Qatil Ki Talash	M. A. Rashid	11-Jul-1986	Successful
Gangwa	Arshad Mirza	23-Aug-1991	Flop

By viewing the aforementioned list, we can perceive that Mumtaz has done many successful films during her film career.

An Offbeat Way of Love

Even after becoming Chaudhry Ajmal's wife, Mumtaz did not abandon her licentiousness. Compelled by her habit, she used to start having affection for others who were coming and going. Chaudhry Ajmal was quite irked by that, yet he kept Mumtaz dear.

One day, Mumtaz went to the studio for the shooting of director Rasheed Akhtar's film. When the shooting concluded, all of a sudden Mumtaz disappeared. After some time had passed, Chaudhry Ajmal asked Rasheed Akhtar about where Mumtaz had gone. Rasheed Akhtar replied, as the shooting had been concluded, everyone from the unit had headed back to their homes. Chaudhry Ajmal did not rely on Rasheed Akhtar's reply because Mumtaz's car was still parked in the studio. Ajmal looked for Mumtaz in every nook and corner of the studio, but he could not find her. All at once, he caught sight of a cabin upstairs. He climbed the stairs and went there, and when he pushed the door forcefully, it opened. What he witnessed is that Mumtaz was lying in an unclothed state while Rasheed Akhtar's assistant (Chuha) was enjoying unrestrained merrymaking. Upon seeing Chaudhry Ajmal, Mumtaz put on her clothes in a topsy-turvy manner and stood up.

Chaudhry Ajmal dragged Mumtaz down the stairs and he was abusing her at the top of his lungs. Listening to those abuses, a lot of people in the studio gathered there. Mumtaz was weeping continuously. She said that Chaudhry Ajmal had been lying. She said that she was worn out and that is why she asked "Chuha" to massage her calves. But Ajmal did not recognize it as truth. He said that his hand fed that whore while she let others gain pleasure from her. He ran to grab a pistol to shoot Mumtaz dead but then she slipped away in her car. Although

Mumtaz got rid of Ajmal that day, he made Mumtaz's supervision strict. Despite that, Mumtaz used to find one way or another to satisfy her heart.

Mumtaz and Nadeem

Nadeem is a single actor who has been popular among the public since 1976 to the present day. Merely his name is considered enough as an assurance for a film to become successful. Nadeem has made his art acknowledged through his great performances in both Urdu and Punjabi films.

As has been mentioned in the previous pages, Mumtaz was fond of watching films from her childhood. Nadeem's first film, "Chakori," was released on 19 May 1967 and its director was Ehtisham, who later became his father-in-law as well. Nadeem acted well in this film. When Mumtaz watched this film in the cinema hall, she became Nadeem's fan. His reflection was stuck in her head. When Mumtaz grew up and signed for her first film, "Ehsas," her luck became spectacular as Nadeem was also a part of that film. Although in the film "Ehsas," Mumtaz's encounters with Nadeem were minimal, she was dancing out of happiness. The film "Ehsas" was released on 22 December 1972.

After that, director S. Suleman agreed with Nadeem and Shabnam to make a film, "Intezar." Mumtaz also got a lively role in this film. Nadeem and Shabnam love each other in this film, whereas Mumtaz is in one-sided love with Nadeem. During the shooting of this film, Nadeem was greatly fascinated by Mumtaz. During the entire film shooting, he kept presuming that Mumtaz was acting well – but she was showing affection for Nadeem for real. Nadeem could not see Mumtaz's impatience and he also became her captive in love.

It is during those days when Mumtaz was married to Ajmal. Nadeem and Mumtaz's love began thriving in the studio. They started meeting each other stealthily. Afterwards, they booked a room in a hotel. When Chaudhry Ajmal found out about their maturing love, he imposed further strict supervision over Mumtaz but all his efforts went in vain. At last, being vexed, he arranged a film ceremony in which Nadeem was to be made to drink Mumtaz's defiled milk so that they would both become like siblings. During that ceremony, when Mumtaz had drunk half a glass of milk, then Ajmal brought that glass to Nadeem to which he refused to drink. He compelled Nadeem to drink that milk by showing his pistol and later, Ajmal announced that Nadeem and Mumtaz were brother and sister to each other thenceforth. Ajmal Chaudhry was extremely certain that from now on they would both keep from having a love affair but that only remained his unfulfilled longing. This is because a few days later, they were busy having unrestrained merrymaking and someone informed Ajmal about it.

Upon hearing this news, he became quite worrisome as all his strategies had concluded in failure. After this incident, Ajmal's brothers forced him to leave that 'prostitute'. Ultimately, after the completion of the film "Sheeshy Ka Ghar," Ajmal divorced

Mumtaz. Take note that this film was released on 2 June 1978. Its director was Nazar ul Islam.

After Mumtaz, Nadeem's name was also associated with Saira Naseem and Atiqa Odho but these scenarios did not gain much notoriety. Let's examine a list of some of Nadeem's Nigar Award-winning films.

Some of Nadeem's Award-winning films

Title of Film	Director	Release Date	Outcome
Chakori	Ehtisham	19-May-1967	Won Nigar Award & Successful
Ehsas	Nazar ul Islam	22-Dec-1972	"
Sharafat	Nazar ul Islam	7-Aug-1974	"
Aina	Nazar ul Islam	18-Mar-1977	"
Play Boy	Shamim Ara	5-Sep-1978	"
Qurbani	Pervaiz Malik	22-May-1981	"
Sangdill	Hasan Tariq	2-Apr-1982	"
Dehleez	Javed Fazil	23-Apr-1983	"
Choroun Ki Baat	Iqbal Kashmiri	29-May-1987	"
Bazar e Husn	Javed Fazil	9-Sep-1988	"
Bulandi	Javed Fazil	21-Sep-1990	"
Gori Diyan Jhanjran	Javed Fazil	19-Jan-1990	"
Watan Ke Rakhwale	Hasnain	23-Jun-1991	"
Jeeva	Syed Noor	3-Mar-1995	"
Madam Rani	Masood Butt	10-May-1995	"
Diwane Tere Pyar Ke	Syed Noor	7-Nov-1997	"

The aforementioned list of a few of Nadeem's films must have produced an impression on you that Nadeem did not let the graph of success decline.

Mumtaz and Raheel Bari

Bari Malik was a film distributor, apart from being an owner of the studio. Long ago, he had married an early actress, Najma. From her womb were born Raheel Bari, Khurram Bari and Zarq Bari. After that, he married an actress, Saloni, from whom he had a daughter. And two years prior, that girl had gotten married to Ilyas Kashmiri's son.

Raheel Bari became the owner of Bari Studio after his father left for Dubai. He was a married man yet he was inclined towards streetwalkers. After getting divorced from Ajmal, Mumtaz was floating from one place to another aimlessly. Amidst that, she became a friend to Raheel Bari. This relationship continued for several months. Rumors heated up in the studio that both of them had got married but Mumtaz and Raheel refuted them. Mumtaz's ulterior motive to befriend Raheel was to become an owner of the studio, whereas Raheel wanted to enjoy licentiousness by befriending her for just a few days. Both of them were highly driven by their plans.

They both used to accompany each other while going for film shooting. Mumtaz used to get some scenes recorded on set while Raheel stood praising Mumtaz. Haider Chaudhry had cast Mumtaz in his film "Samundar Paar," and its shooting was settled to take place in London. But Mumtaz did not want to go to London without anyone accompanying her. Later on, she agreed to go with Raheel to London.

They both departed for London for the shooting of the film "Samundar Paar." There, they analyzed each other closely. After the completion of the film, they arrived in Pakistan and made an announcement of their marriage. Take note that "Samundar Paar" was released on 19 August 1983.

After publicizing their marriage, they started living happily. After a while, Raheel realized that Mumtaz was still pretending to love every passerby. One day they had a big argument over this matter, but a few days later their friends made efforts to reconcile them.

After reconciliation, their love became elevated to an emotional level. Mumtaz even used to take Raheel along her to the red-light district. And he also used to roam the market cheerfully in the daylight. Many people in the film industry were bewildered by this incident that on one hand, Raheel had married a girl from the red-light district, while on the other, he did not forsake going to the market. But Raheel did not pay attention to any of that chatter.

Meanwhile, Mumtaz began taking over the studio according to her plan. Mumtaz started sitting in Raheel's office in Bari Studio for the most part, then. She herself used to collect rent for the studio and Raheel had also given her a great deal of leniency concerning matters of the studio. It was Mumtaz who used to inspect the bookkeeping of the studio. When Raheel asked Mumtaz to get a new air conditioner installed in the projection hall, she immediately acted upon it.

Besides that, she herself bought new equipment for the office. Mumtaz was handling the expenditures as an owner of the studio, whereas Raheel was giving Mumtaz a flap with a fox tail. Coming under the heading of Mumtaz's various expenditures, 3 million rupees got spent, which she spent with free will.

After these expenditures, Raheel started to pull away gradually from Mumtaz. He began fighting on every petty issue. He often used to threaten Mumtaz with divorce. Mumtaz then realized that in her pursuit of becoming an owner of the studio, she had lost her 3 million rupees as well. At last, Raheel divorced Mumtaz.

After her divorce, Mumtaz remained distressed for many years. She discontinued working in films as well. After a course of a few years, she met a businessman, Khalid Awan. After a relationship of a few months, Mumtaz got married. Nowadays Mumtaz is living with Khalid Awan and resides in America.

Anjuman

MULTAN'S GIFT NO. 1
ANJUMAN

from Multan to England

Multani artists played a great role in the evolution of Pakistan's film industry. Multan has given a myriad of faces to film, who have ruled the film screen. Among them, Suraiya Multani, Shakeela Qureshi, Naheed Akhtar, Gori, Anjuman, Saima, Reema, Sana, Saira Khan, and Noor are included. They were born in Multan. In this book, three gifts of Multan will be mentioned among which Anjuman, Reema and Saima will be listed respectively. These three have ruled the film industry from 1979 to date.

It is remarked about Anjuman that in the red-light district of Multan, a beautiful baby girl was born. Nawal Deen named her "Anjum." Anjum's mother expired during her childhood. Her aunt Nazeeran brought her up. Afterwards, she made it well known that Anjum is her own daughter. A few years later a fair-complexioned girl was born at the place of Anjum's aunt, whom they named Gohar (Gori). The populace is of the view that Gori and Anjum are sisters.

Their condition is similar to that of Sangeeta and Kavita. According to the tradition of the red-light district, Anjum was trained in dance and music. In a course of a few years, Anjum (Anjuman) became a tall, slender and enchanting girl. She had a beautiful voice which was pleasing to the ears.

Anjum was eager to become an actress. There were no resources available in Multan to fulfill her interest. Her family members left Multan and settled in the red-light district of Lahore. Anjum earned a decent income in the markets of Lahore. Plenty of landlords, high born men and industrialists became victims of Anjum's love. Being entrapped in the vortex of Anjum's tresses, they kept opening their vaults and Anjum kept growing her bank balance.

To further increase her income, Anjum made tours to Arab countries as well, which were highly profitable. Anjum was a Sheikh's mistress for four years in the United Arab Emirates, and he loaded Anjum with gold. Being ensnared by the love of the tall charmer, the Sheikh did not let any other maiden get close to him for many years. Take note that at one time, he adored Babra Shareef as well.

Entry in Films

As Anjum had earned a sufficient income in the red-light district, that is why she bought a bungalow in Gulberg.

According to her plan, Anjum bought her bungalow next to Muhammad Ali and Zeba's house. In filmdom, Mr. Muhammad Ali was regarded with honor and he had a strong influence as well. That is why Anjum started visiting Muhammad Ali's house. Anjum told Muhammad Ali that she was a landlord's daughter in Multan. She said that her family was well off and that money was the grime on their hands. Mr. Muhammad Ali was quite fascinated by this conversation. One day Anjum asked Muhammad Ali to get her work in a film and a few days after that, Muhammad Ali introduced Anjum to a filmmaker and director, Shabab Keranvi. Shabab Keranvi renamed Anjum to Anjuman.

Anjuman did not accept any wages for her first film, "Wade Ki Zanjeer." Moreover, she spent her own capital on the film along with Shabab Keranvi, so that Muhammad Ali and Shabab Keranvi become assured that Anjuman belonged to a big landlord family. "Wade Ki Zanjeer" was released on 4 February 1979. Apart from Anjuman, Muhammad Ali and Waheed Murad also starred in the film. Anjuman acted unreservedly in the film. To paint a realistic picture of romantic scenes, she became so close to Waheed Murad that he also became infatuated with Anjuman like Muhammad Ali did.

It was Muhammad Ali and Waheed Murad's joint opinion that Anjuman would have a brilliant future. But Anjuman's first film, "Wade Ki Zanjeer," was a bad flop. Anjuman's second film, "Dou Raste," was released on 25 May 1979 which was also a flop. Its director was Shabab Keranvi as well.

Anjuman had an agreement of three films with Shabab Keranvi. According to this agreement, Anjuman could not work in any other director's film. In light of the agreement, Shabab Keranvi's third film, "Aap Se Kiya Parda," was a comedy film. This film was released on 7 December 1979, it was not a flop but rather moderately successful.

After facing a great deal of trouble, Anjuman succeeded in gaining Shabab Kervani's approval for working in a Punjabi film: "Sardar." This film by director Iqbal Kashmiri was released on 13 August 1980 but as a matter of course, it flopped badly. This way, Anjuman began getting labeled for flop films. It was a disturbing situation for Anjuman. But she did not lose her heart. Rather, she kept striving day and night. She was aware of the fact that the renowned heroine of Punjabi films, Asiya, was not available in filmdom. Hence, she could grab the chance, and afterward, it was proved to be right as circumstances went in Anjuman's favor. Therefore, her efforts did not go in vain.

Anjuman and Younis Malik

Anjuman used to organize dance and music in the red-light district, which attracted many admirers of hers to see her dance. Among her admirers, was a well-known director of Punjabi films, Younis Malik, who was also often spotted in the red-light district.

Younis Malik used to search for new faces for films in the very same the red-light district. One day, while Anjuman was dancing, Younis Malik's and Anjuman's glances met. Anjuman was already waiting in expectation for such a person to come into her life. When the dance was concluded, Anjuman and Younis met in seclusion. During their meeting, Younis offered Anjuman work in a film. Anjuman told Younis Malik that she had signed an agreement on three films with Shabab Keranvi. Once his films were completed, then she would be able to work on other films. But Younis Malik was insistent, so Anjuman promised him that she would meet Shabab Keranvi.

One day, Anjuman surrounded Shabab Keranvi in seclusion. Shabab Keranvi could not escape her seductive eyes and ultimately, he surrendered. At last, he was compelled to let Anjuman work on films by other directors. When Anjuman gave this exciting news to Younis Malik, he cast her in his film "Sher Khan."

In addition to that, director Altaf Hussain cast her in his film "Sala Sahib," director Jahangir Qaiser cast her in the film "Chan Varyam," and director Kaifi cast her in the film "Mile Ga Zulm Da Badla." All four aforementioned films were released on 2 August 1981. All the four films made big bucks, especially "Sala Sahib," "Sher Khan" and "Chan Varyam," which all made a record of achievement. Hence Anjuman was set on her path to success.

Anjuman's First Scandal

The actor Asif Raza Meer worked in both television and films as a hero. Asif's first film, "Prince," which was directed by S. Suleman, released on 30 June 1978.

Anjuman's first film scandal was with Asif Raza Meer. What happened was that one day on the film set, Anjuman said who would feed her and Asif Raza Meer's children.

The next day, newspapers gave wide publicity to this statement. Afterward, Anjuman denied it but those who were well aware of the circumstances remarked that this incident was true. Anjuman said that Asif Raza Meer was like a biological brother to her but it was too late.

Nasir Adeeb and Anjuman

Nasir Adeeb was a film writer. He made himself known by writing "Maula Jutt," "Sholay," "Khoon Aur Pani," "Sher Khan," "Badshah," "Khandan," "Jise De Maula," "Hoshiyar" and "Chour Sipahi" etc.

The days came when Anjuman's films were becoming flops and she made every possible effort to gain success, and her eyes fell on Nasir Adeeb. She saw her future prosperity in his nearness. She was well aware of the fact that Nasir Adeeb was an influential personality and he could be of advantage to her.

What happened was that Nasir Adeeb and Anjuman were climbing the stairs to go into the projection hall in the studio.

Nasir was ahead while Anjuman followed him closely while climbing. Nasir stopped there and said, "What is the matter with you? I am a sophisticated, respectable man. I am not used to such antics. Do not ever behave with me in such manner again."

Nasir became so infuriated over this antic of Anjuman, that he made an announcement that in the future he would not write a story or dialogue for any film in which Anjuman would be working.

Later on, a few people made a reconciliation between Anjuman and Nasir Adeeb. Anjuman's plan of entrapping Nasir Adeeb failed badly and furthermore, she was extremely humiliated.

Chaudhry Ismail and Anjuman

Chaudhry Ismail was a flourishing filmmaker and distributor of the Pakistan film industry. He has made some of the best films among which, the following are included:

Title of Film	Director	Release Date
Fraud	Haider Chaudhry	7 July 1977
Sala Sahib	Altaf Hussain	2 August 1981
Rustam Te Khan	Altaf Hussain	25 November 1983
Dhi Rani	Altaf Hussain	9 April 1985

Anjuman worked for the first time with Chaudhry Ismail in the film "Sala Sahib." Anjuman was very mindful of Chaudhry Ismail being a well-off person. Therefore, she planned to entrap Mr. Chaudhry.

Chaudhry Ismail had set up his production office in Ever New Studio. All kinds of equipment was available there. When Anjuman was free after the day's film shooting, she would sit in that office. Those days it became famous in the studio that Anjuman was fond of Chaudhry Ismail's office. Anjuman made it a daily ritual to go to the office. The situation reached a point where whenever Mr. Ismail was present in the office, Anjuman would show up there. It became a prevalent notion in filmdom that Anjuman and Chaudhry Ismail wished to tie the marital knot. When this news reached Chaudhry Ismail, he called Anjuman and pleaded with her to leave him alone. He told her that he was a married man, had kids and that being a businessman he could not afford to enjoy such licentiousness. He also told her that earlier he was associated with the actress Asiya as well, which he had denied at the time. When Anjuman sensed Chaudhry Ismail's scrupulous behavior, she herself left him alone.

Jamaat Ali Shah, Anjuman and Gul Khan

In 1981, on one hand, Anjuman's successful films were being released while on the other she was having entanglements with Jamaat Ali Shah and Gul Khan. Jamaat Ali Shah was a middle-aged industrialist. Since he had a superabundance of money, he thought of amusing himself in the last flush of his life. Anjuman established a love affair with Jamaat Shah to the fullest extent. To pay in return, Jamaat Shah also squandered his saved money.

On the other hand, Anjuman was expressing her love for a Pashtun, Gul Khan, as well. Mr. Khan was also highly enamored of Anjuman. He also spent on Anjuman extravagantly. Anjuman was dedicating a greater chunk of her time to Jamaat Ali Shah as he was a more affluent man. Finally, Anjuman and Jamaat Ali Shah's love affair was realized and she became pregnant.

Now Anjuman was perturbed lest her news of being pregnant spread in filmdom. So, she made up the excuse of going abroad for a trip and deferred the dates of shooting for two months with filmmakers. Even though Anjuman had promised to go for two months, it took her six and a half months to return.

The reason behind such a long time off was that she had to deliver her son through a C-section. For that purpose, she had to get stitches. Anjuman's son was born in 1982. After the birth of her son, Anjuman came to Lahore along with Jamaat Ali Shah on 5 November 1982.

As soon as she arrived in Lahore, she fabricated a convincing excuse that she'd had an appendectomy. She did that to keep the world of filmdom from being suspicious of her. But those who had an insight could easily figure out what had happened with her abroad. This way, Anjuman gave birth to a son three years later after entering filmdom.

Being distraught by Anjuman and Jamaat Ali Shah's close relationship, Gul Khan committed suicide. That is how Anjuman propelled her true love to confront death for the sake of gaining riches. It was the irony of fate that on one hand there was lying Gul Khan's lifeless body while on the other, Anjuman was receiving an award for the best heroine in the film "Sher Khan."

Muhammad Sarwar Bhatti and Anjuman

Muhammad Sarwar Bhatti earned his name and fame by making the film "Maula Jutt." "Maula Jutt" set new records of success. From February 11, 1979 to 1981, fans of the film "Maula Jutt" did not allow any other movie to be screened in the Shabistan Cinema Lahore.

When a renowned heroine of Punjabi films, Asiya, had left the film industry, finding a new Punjabi heroine became a conundrum for filmmakers.

After the success of "Maula Jutt," one day Muhammad Sarwar Bhatti announced making a film, "Chan Varyam." In quest of a heroine, he often used to visit the red-light district.

One day he reached Anjuman's brothel. She was having an dance when he arrived. Mr. Sarwar Bhatti kept gazing at her in wonder. He told his friend Gohar that the girl was beautiful but it seems he had seen her before. He said that he failed to recollect where he had seen her. Sarwar Bhatti's friend had a brilliant presence of mind and he said to him that he might have seen her in the film "Vade Ki Zanjeer." Sarwar Bhatti was saddened to hear that along with working in films this girl danced as a prostitute as well.

Long story cut short: when the dance concluded, Sarwar Bhatti asked Anjuman why she danced as a prostitute. She replied that it was her compulsion to dance. She said that she herself despised that work. It was not something that decent people would do. She also said that she was an honorable girl from Multan and someone had pushed her into that filthy swamp. Sarwar Bhatti was quite grief-stricken after hearing Anjuman's conversation. To consolidate partnership with Anjuman, he gave her a chance in the film "Chan Varyam" as a heroine. Anjuman promised Sarwar Bhatti that she would not dance numbers again, but she used to keep running her shady business in the background.

Sarwar Bhatti started visiting Anjuman's house repeatedly. It made Anjuman and her mother quite delighted because he was like a goose that lays golden eggs. Anjuman's mother told Sarwar Bhatti on several occasions, "O son, consider it your own house. Feel free to come here."

Anjuman and Sarwar Bhatti kept meeting inside and outside the studio and sang songs of love to each other. After "Maula Jutt" became a hit film, Sarwar Bhatti made good earnings which he started spending on Anjuman afterward. This story which began with love was about to lay the foundations for marriage. Anjuman said to Sarwar Bhatti that she would marry only him, otherwise, she would remain unmarried for her whole life.

When "Chan Varyam" was released on 2 August 1981, it was publicized all over Pakistan. Sarwar Bhatti earned millions from this film, almost as good as "Maula Jutt." Now Sarwar Bhatti started lending aid to Anjuman open-heartedly. And along with that, He presented the demand for marriage. Apart from Anjuman's film "Chan Varyam," "Sala Sahib" and "Sher Khan" had also set a record business. It made eminent filmmakers and directors pursue Anjuman.

When Anjuman realized this situation, she started to withdraw from Sarwar Bhatti. This incident made him dispirited. For an intervening time, he left Anjuman and started making a new film. In this film, Khanum was cast as a substitute for Anjuman. This was to make her realize that she had wronged Bhatti.

Masood Parvez was the director of the film "Mirza Jutt," which was released on 28 September 1982. This film of Sarwar Bhatti flopped badly. Mr. Bhatti became gloomy but Anjuman's "Muft Barse," "Dhi Rani" and "Rustam Te Khan" set a record of success.

After the film flopped, Sarwar Bhatti began pursuing Anjuman one more time. If Anjuman had some free time, she would spend a few moments with Sarwar Bhatti. But now nothing remained the same, as Anjuman was also disheartened upon being not cast in "Mirza Jutt." Sarwar Bhatti was quite mournful over this situation. He mustered up some courage and made one more film, "Haq Meharbani," which was released on 18 November 1985. Its director was Iftikhar Khan and in this film too, another heroine was cast in Anjuman's place. This means that Babra Shareef was cast in the film and it flopped as well.

Sarwar Bhatti felt highly dejected and he adopted seclusion. He thought that he had shamed himself by loving a prostitute. He was accustomed to using profane language about Anjuman for hours while being in the company of his friends.

Now he remained idle for most of the time, while Anjuman indulged in the world of filmdom to such an extent that she did not even bother inquiring about him. Sarwar Bhatti's friends used to console him and advised to not grieve, as Allah is Merciful. They used to encourage him to come out of the claws of that illness and to make a film on the topic of prostitutes.

Sarwar Bhatti approved of this idea and he selected Salma Agha for the film. The reason that led to this selection was that Salma Agha was an inherited prostitute. And that is why she could perform the role of a prostitute exceptionally.

Earlier, Hasan Tariq had made "Suraiya Bhopali," "Tehzeeb," "Umrao Jaan Ada" and "Anjuman" etc., on the topic of prostitutes. He was also in love from head to toe with Rani. But Rani had humiliated Hasan Tariq extremely in the last stage of his life. For that reason, Hasan Tariq also made a film, "Sangdill," as a slap in Rani's face before his death. Babra Shareef played the central role in "Sangdill." This film was released on 12 April 1982 and it gained massive success.

Sarwar Bhatti made director Javed Fazil make a film with the title "Bazar e Husn." In this film, Nadeem played the role of Hasan Tariq and Nadeem was also named Tariq in the film.

"Bazar e Husn" was released on 9 September 1988. In addition to making big bucks, this film won many awards. Even though Sarwar Bhatti's film gained success, Anjuman had now become estranged from him. After "Bazar e Husn," Sarwar Bhatti announced making another film, "Lakhpal Daku," but till now its shooting could not be started.

Anjuman and Sultan Rahi

Anjuman and Sultan Rahi's onscreen pairing was a hit in Punjabi films. Whenever Anjuman and Sultan Rahi were in a film together, fans would rush towards the cinemas. This onscreen couple gave numerous successful films to the filmdom among which "Sala Sahib," "Sher Khan," "Chan Varyam," "Dhi Rani," "Rustam Te Khan," Dara Baloch," Lagan," "Do Beegha Zameen" and "Sholay" are included.

Prior to mentioning Anjuman and Sultan Rahi, I will write in detail solely about Sultan Rahi.

Sultan Rahi

Sultan Rahi was born in Rawalpindi. The yearning to work in films brought him to Lahore. Sultan Rahi's first film, "Baghi," was released on 14 September 1956. Its director was Ishfaq Malik. In the initial period, Sultan Rahi used to work on stage in addition to working in films. Sultan Rahi used to act in a stage drama along with Nanha and Rangeela in the Lahore Railway Burt Hall.

When Sultan Rahi started working in films, he was destitute of money. He did not even have the fare in his pockets to reach the studio. He used to travel by means of actor Raj Multani's cycle. For a number of years, he kept himself limited to insignificant characters. At that time, Sultan Rahi also used to work as a day laborer for 3 rupees.

It is a matter of those days when Sultan Rahi used to get this kind of role. For example, a film was released on 15 June 1962 and its director was Farukh Bukhari. In the whole film, Sultan Rahi had just one dialogue to deliver, i.e. "Yes, sir." Similarly, director Ashraf Khan's film "Chaudah Saal" was released on 19 April 1968. In this film, Sultan Rahi only prepared a hookah for smoking and his role in the film ended.

For a few years, Sultan Rahi worked as a fighter as well. But he did not lose courage as he had learned to rely on hard work. He was certain that one day he would become a great hero. Director Iqbal Kashmiri announced about making a film, "Babul." An energetic villain was required in the film and after giving a lot of thought, he cast Sultan Rahi in it. When this film was released on 18 June 1971, then Mazhar Shah, who was a well-known villain in those days, slipped from the minds of people.

Similarly, Aslam Dar made a Punjabi film named "Basheera." In this film, Sultan Rahi was presented with Basheera Daku's character. When "Basheera" was released on 21 July 1972, everywhere "Basheera, Basheera, and Basheera Daku" reverberated. The dialogues delivered in this film are imprinted on the minds of people to this day. Sultan Rahi's death scene at the end is the crux of this film.

Especially memorable is Sultan Rahi's line: "Take your hand off this sedan chair, you lying Chaudhry! The sisters whose brothers are alive, even death cannot interrupt their sedan chair."

After "Basheera," a number of films lined up for Sultan Rahi… among those were "Bala Gujjar," "Zarq Khan," "Pehla Waar," "Ustad" and "Khanan De Khan Paroney" are included.

Ahmed Nadeem Qasmi wrote a fable named "Gandasa." Hasan Askari picked up Gandasa's character from that fable and made a Punjabi film, "Wehshi Jutt," from it. The film was released on 8 August 1975 and was a big success. After that, Sultan Rahi was showered with film offers. Amidst this shower, director Younis Malik's film "Maula Jutt" was screened in Shabistan Cinema Lahore on 11 February 1979. This film was screened in Shabistan Cinema Lahore for a course of two years.

Sultan Rahi worked in more than 500 films. He was an excellent actor, human, friend and individual. There was a time when he used to go to the studio by means of Raj Multani's cycle. And he witnessed such a time as well when he had a queue of cars lined up, and his children were seeking education in America.

Sultan Rahi on the Paths of Romance

Sultan Rahi was a two-faced man. On one hand, he used to give aid to the poor, getting mosques constructed, while on the other, he was inclined to mundane love. Let's analyze Sultan Rahi's romantic life.

Actress Zamurd

Zamurd, a fairy of the red-light district, had plenty of courtships in the world of filmdom. Among them, Shahid, Shammi Malik, director Amin Malik, and filmmaker Ahad Malik are included. Those days when Sultan Rahi was appearing as a hero in films, he fell for Zamurd. It was the same period when she had been rejected by Shahid and she was in dire need of support. Sultan Rahi proceeded with this love affair with great wariness.

It is because he proved to be a noble man in filmdom, but Zamurd made Sultan Rahi enjoy licentiousness open-heartedly. This love affair did not turn into marriage because on one hand, Sultan Rahi was a father while on the other he did not want to make his wife go against him. For this reason, this courtship continued furtively for a long period.

Meena Chaudhry

Meena Chaudhry was a dancer. Oftentimes, she used to get her scenes recorded as a club dancer and dancer as a prostitute. She belonged to the red-light district.

Those days when Sultan Rahi was struggling to make a mark in films, Meena Chaudhry entered his life. To make a name for himself in filmdom, Sultan Rahi strived for almost 15 years. Meena Chaudhry could not wait such a long term. One day she got married in secrecy to a goldsmith from Multan, and bid farewell to the filmdom and Sultan Rahi to reside in Multan.

Sultan Rahi felt quite dejected by this incident as Meena Chaudhry had been his friend through rough times when he did not even own a single cycle.

Meena Chaudhry had worked in films like "Mulaqat," "Eid Mubarak," "Sharabi," "Parchayen," "Pag Teri Hath Mera," etc.

Asiya

Asiya was a well-known actress in Pakistani Punjabi films. In 1970, Shabab Keranvi had cast her in his film "Insan Aur Admi." Afterward, Riaz Shahid cast her in "Gharnata" and Rangeela cast her in "Dil Aur Dunya." Asiya's domestic name was Firdaus, it was Riaz Shahid who named her Asiya. Asiya had moved from the Market of Karachi to Lahore. She was a quite flirtatious lady, which is why she had numerous scandals.

These include:

1. Actor Rangeela
2. Actor Khalifa Nazeer Ahmed
3. Licentious nights with Arab princes

4. Bari Malik (owner of Bari Studio)
5. Actor Asif Khan
6. Cameraman Riaz Butt (she was caught red-handed in a bathroom)
7. Filmmaker Chaudhry Ismail
8. Actor Mahmood Khan (the hero in the film "April Fool")
9. Filmmaker and director Riaz Shahid
10. Seth Farooq

She married Seth Farooq from Karachi and fled to Hong Kong. In recompense for this marriage, Asiya's maternal uncle received 1.5 million rupees from Seth Farooq.

Asiya appeared with Sultan Rahi in a number of films. These include "Vehshi Jutt," Ultimatum," "Jagga Gujjar," "Lahori Badshah," "Shareef Badmash," "Boycott," "Goga Sher," "Vehshi Gujjar" and "Maula Jutt."

Sultan Rahi was involved in a one-sided love with Asiya. She did not use to be apathetic towards him as she already had scores of lovers. Furthermore, she did not consider him merited. To work with Sultan Rahi in films was her compulsion for the sake of business. But Sultan Rahi was so defiant that one-day Asiya reciprocated with love. But it only remained an unfulfilled desire for him.

After the success of "Maula Jutt," director Younis Malik announced making another film, "Maula Jutt in London." It was released on 27 November 1981 and its unit went to London for film shooting.

Both Sultan Rahi and Asiya were also present in this unit. One day, Sultan Rahi approached Asiya in seclusion and expressed his love for her.

At first, Asiya listened to his conversation but later on, she disgraced Sultan Rahi a lot. She said to Sultan Rahi that she could love a dog but not him. After listening to what Asiya had said, Sultan Rahi rushed towards his room in the hotel, for the reason that the people of the unit started gathering there after listening to Asiya's loud voice.

Apart from Asiya, Sultan Rahi used to recommend new coming girls as well in the final days of his life. He suggested that they should be given a chance in films. When actress Saima appeared as a newbie in films, Sultan Rahi recommended Saima to many directors. One day, even Anjuman took umbrage at this. He had illicit relationships with many other actresses as well. Those include Saima, Shehzadi and Babra Raj's scandal as well.

Anjuman and Sultan Rahi's Films

Anjuman and Sultan Rahi's onscreen couple was considered an assurance for a Punjabi film to succeed. Sultan Rahi was proficient in performing characters who were brusque, callous and combatant. Whereas Anjuman used to accompany Sultan

Rahi as an innocent attractive girl, Punjab's Jutti, a stunning belle.

Sultan Rahi and Anjuman's Collective Films

Film Title	Director	Release Date
Sher Khan	Younis Malik	2-Aug-81
Sala Sahib	Altaf Hussain	2-Aug-81
Chan Varyam	Jahangir Qaiser	2-Aug-81
Sholay	Younis Malik	11-May-84
Qeemat	Haider Chaudhry	31-Oct-86
Doli Te Hathkari	Safdar Hussain	6-Feb-87
Hunterwali	Iqbal Kashmiri	9-Dec-88
Super Girl	M. Aslam	27-Jan-89
Kalka	Shahid Rana	7-May-89
Kali Charan	Khalifa	27-Apr-90
Chiragh Bali	Masood Butt	23-Jun-91
Majhoo	Masood Butt	12-Jun-91
Bala Peeray Wala	Masood Butt	4-Nov-94
Golden Girl	Hasnain	10-Nov-95

Besides Anjuman, Sultan Rahi worked with Asiya, Kavita, Saima, Neeli, Nadira, Sapna, Sangeeta, Gori, etc. as well.

Sultan Rahi's Assassination

Sultan Rahi was assassinated in front of Pasban Kanday, which is in the suburb of Gujranwala city, on 9 January 1996. The news of his murder spread like wildfire all over Pakistan. Such an actor, who was beloved to commoners, and was a hero of the city of poor, had departed them forever. People used to visit cinemas only for the sake of watching Sultan Rahi's films. No matter which heroine acted in a film with Sultan Rahi, the film would be a hit. Owing to his thunderous voice, Sultan Rahi ruled the hearts of the people from 1956 to 1996.

Motives Behind the Assassination

The motives behind Sultan Rahi's assassination involve his secretary, Haji Ahsan Iqbal. Haji Ahsan had been serving Sultan Rahi for the long term as his secretary. A few years prior, he borrowed 4 million rupees from Sultan Rahi to make a film. With the cooperation of director Jahangir Mughal, he made a film named "Zabata." In this film, Babra Shareef acted as a heroine. It was a long-winded film. One scene used to remain on screen for such a prolonged time that it would lead the spectators to be struck by boredom.

"Zabata" was released on 3 September 1993. Its protraction and ill-timed action caused it to flop. Haji Ahsan had borne a tremendous loss due to this film. As Sultan Rahi had given a loan to Haji Ahsan for making a film, so he demanded paying 4 million rupees back to him. In those days, Sultan Rahi had planned about setting up a factory in Muzaffargarh and he was in dire need of money, while on the other hand, Haji Ahsan would always shirk it.

As Sultan Rahi was a chaser of alluring girls, so taking advantage of this, one day Haji Ahsan took him to his niece, Saima. He made them have a prolonged meeting. His niece, Saima, was a cunning girl. She grasped Sultan Rahi through her deceptions. It became routine for Sultan Rahi to be at Saima's house. A few months later, Saima told Sultan Rahi that she was pregnant. This news was perplexing for Sultan Rahi. Long story cut short: she became a mother to a beautiful son.

Now, Sultan Rahi was burdened with his son's load as well as Saima. That is why he reduced the amount of 4 million as a return for his loan. Haji Ahsan had also gathered plenty of wealth from Sultan Rahi and exploited him through Saima. As Saima was a cunning girl, she had made Sultan Rahi transfer ample property into her name. Yet it did not diminish Haji Ahsan and Saima's desire for more. One day, Haji Ahsan suggested to Sultan Rahi that he should get Saima and her son settled in America, so that this story would come to a conclusion.

Sultan Rahi agreed to Haji Ahsan's suggestion. In this regard, Haji Ahsan gave a reference from former Prime Minister's Secretary Naheed Khan that he was on good terms with them. And that he would assist him in getting a visa for America very soon.

He said that he would have to accompany him to Islamabad. Sultan Rahi went along with him to Islamabad. But they could not meet Naheed Khan. Sultan Rahi wanted to stay for one more day in Islamabad. But Haji Ahsan was persistent on returning to Lahore in any case, as a film shooting was due the next day. So Sultan Rahi agreed upon going back.

On their way back Haji Ahsan pulled over in the suburbs of Gujranwala. He did so as an excuse to check the car and in the blink of an eye, two masked men appeared on the spot and killed Sultan Rahi.

This way, Haji Ahsan saved himself from returning 4 million rupees, while in addition to that, he encroached on the whole property that had been transferred in his niece's name. Police have not solved this murder to date.

Anjuman Marries Mubeen Malik

Mubeen Malik was gallant man and a businessman. He often used to visit the red-light district. As he worked for the Income Tax Department, for this reason prostitutes did not want to ruin their relationship with him.

Before Anjuman, actress Nadira had also been in wedlock with him. In the days when Anjuman was striving to entrap him in her love, he was employed by the government's tax recovery department. It was the same when Anjuman had to pay many of her dues to the department. He often used to go to Anjuman's house to watch her perform dance, and listen to songs. Then when leaving, he used to demand the payment of dues to the department. Out of fear of investigation, Anjuman served him well. Anjuman's mother was initially disdainful to Mubeen Malik but when it was revealed to her that Anjuman had to pay many of her dues to the department, her heart softened. She started calling him a son.

Eventually, the son showed his true nature and got married to Anjuman. All the customs were celebrated with pageantry. In the filmdom of Lahore, this marriage ceremony is considered among the best ones. After marriage, their honeymoon began, and it lasted for a year. Filmmakers in Lahore were awaiting Anjuman's return so their film shootings could be completed. It was during their honeymoon period that there started to occur minor conflicts between Anjuman and Mubeen Malik. At last, amid these disputes, Anjuman gave birth to a son.

After the birth of her son, when Anjuman went back to the studio, she appeared strikingly different. Her body had become heavy and clumsy, and along with that, her face had widened as well.

Meanwhile, Mubeen Malik was making statements that Anjuman would not be working in films anymore. Earlier, Mubeen Malik had also insisted Nadira should discontinue working in films, which later on took the shape of a divorce.

Anjuman also started making public statements against Mubeen Malik and in such an attempt, she said that Mubeen Malik wanted to throw acid on her. She also said that he had been giving her sleeping pills which were making her overweight and her legs were often in pain. She said that Mubeen Malik's friends came over to her place in an intoxicated state and harassed her. Besides that, Mubeen Malik also asked for her jewelry, cash and cars and labeled her as a prostitute of the red-light district.

The conflicts became prolonged and during these circumstances, a baby girl was born to Anjuman. This further aggravated the situation and the matter went to court. Mubeen Malik said that as Anjuman was a prostitute, her character traits were not good. He also said that her sister Gori was a dancer as well and her brother was also sentenced in a heroin case, which is why he wanted to keep his children away from their influence.

The court made the decision that as children were young then, that is why they would stay with their mother (Anjuman) but Mubeen Malik would be able to meet them on the last Thursday of every month, from 2 o'clock to 4 o' clock.

By cause of children, they were bound to meet each other. Gradually, their dispute turned into affection which led to their reconciliation. On this wise, Mubeen Malik gave up on the idea of divorce and they started their life afresh.

Gori and Anjuman

Anjuman and Gori grew young in the same household. Although their biological mothers were different, still they used to consider each other sisters. Gori commenced her career in film with director Nazar Shabab's film, "Zara Si Baat," which was released on 31 December 1982. She acted in numerous films after this film but could not become an essential star in the industry by the same token that Anjuman did.

Most of Gori's films are also with Sultan Rahi, among her famous films "Nagin," "Jogi," "Nangi Talwar," "Shera Pandi," "Falak Sher," "Badmash Thug," "Supergirl," "Gandasa," "Sher Dill," "Pattan" and "Roshan Jutt" are included. Gori worked in almost 60 films.

The reason that led to Gori working in films was her dances. Renowned landowners, nobility and politicians were fans of her dance numbers. A few years ago, Gori had been arrested while dancing, and police took her to the police station. After going to the police station, when Gori threatened that she would submit the names of all the people who used to visit her brothel in the press that day, the officers of the police department released her immediately.

Anjuman and Gori also used to have some disputes at home. Once upon a time, Anjuman said about Gori and her mother in the press that she had no relation with them and she belonged to a noble family. She also said that they were louts. Upon hearing this, Gori also started giving statements against her. In the continuation of these incidents, Gori occupied Anjuman's bungalow (Gulberg 36G).

Anjuman had gone to London now, but her grief for her bungalow followed her there and did not let her sleep in peace.

Anjuman and Her Sexy Character

After her marriage, when Anjuman resumed working in films, she had become heavy and clumsy. Her value in the market was diminishing as well. On the other hand, Neeli and Nadira had attracted filmmakers towards them.

In contrast, Kavita and Babra Shareef were getting their scenes recorded semi-naked. Anjuman pondered that she should also adopt modernity. In director Kaifi's film, "Bilawal," Anjuman was given a pretty and diaphanous dress. Anjuman had to get a song recorded by being wet in the rain wearing that dress. The filmmaker had also made gold buttons studded on her top.

Anjuman thought that if she left her upper buttons unfastened, then that would look great. She insisted the director Kaifi act upon it. During the shooting, the whole unit was getting amused by seeing Anjuman's alluring body behind those unfastened buttons. "Bilawal" was released on 7 May 1989.

The film gained high recognition – rather the song with unfastened buttons became a super hit. When this news reached the higher authorities, they canceled the license of the film "Bilawal" for six months. Six months later, when this film was released again, the censor had omitted the rain song.

Anjuman's Third Film and Setting out for London

After marriage, due to her conflict with Mubeen Malik, Anjuman did not sign to any film for a duration of almost five to six years. When for the third time, Anjuman intended to work in films, she was cordially welcomed in the studio. Mr. Maulana Akram Awan launched the film "Chaudhrani."

Newspapers all over the country wrote columns over the matter, raising their objections and asking why a religious leader had inaugurated a film.

Filmmaker Zulfiqar Ali Mana and director Hasan Askari's film was released on 12 November 1999. The film was able to make big bucks. After the success of the film, filmmakers analogized Anjuman's return as a good omen. At the age of 40, Anjuman revealed her desire to act as a heroine in films as well. But film experts were of the view that Anjuman had grown old then and that she would not be able to assert herself as the best heroine. But Anjuman was persistent that she was still ruling the hearts of commoners.

After "Chaudhrani," a list of Anjuman's flopped films goes like this:

Film Title	Director	Release Date	Outcome
Jag Mahi	Pervaiz Rana	9 January 2000	Flopped
Peengan	Kaifi	4 February 2000	Flopped
Jatti Da Vair	Perwaiz Rana	28 July 2000	Flopped
Aik Dhi Punjab Di	Kaifi	9 September 2000	Flopped

After her films were unceasing flops, Anjuman became worn out with the film industry. For her whole life, she had earned through films and several other carnival activities but she made up her mind to bid farewell to the film industry.

Anjuman sold her property including her bungalow, car, gold jewelry and precious items to buy pounds. She did so to not face any trouble regarding currency in London. She emigrated to London on 16 September 2000.

Now, she is residing with her husband and children in London. She has also set up a dance academy. In addition to that, she has bought a hotel consisting of 32 rooms, and a restaurant in Black Beach Pool. She also has a slot in a TV channel where she can promote Pakistani culture. Now, her children are also getting an education in the schools of London.

Prior to Anjuman's departure from the country, the late Sultan Rahi's family also got settled in America. Sultan Rahi's sons said that their father's murderers are still at large in the country but no one was arrested. That is why they would not return to it.

Anjuman has no regrets about leaving the country; the only thing she grieves about is that bungalow that Gori seized. When Anjuman entered the film industry, four consecutive flop films had adjudged her ill-omened. They were "Vade Ki Zanjeer," "Do Raste," "Aap Se Kiya Parda" and "Sardar." At the time of leaving the industry, she again had four flops in her lot, "Peengan," "Aik Dhi Punjab Di," "Jatti Da Vair" and "Jag Mahi." That is why it is said history repeats itself.

Reema

MULTAN'S GIFT NO. 2
REEMA

Her Name Holds its Worth

Reema's maternal grandfather, Khushi Muhammad, had come from Amritsar to Multan. He made his abode in the red-light district's Gul Road. When Khushi Muhammad's daughter Saiyan Arsa Cheema entered puberty, she started giving herself airs. Along with being into music and dance, having ever new love affairs was her favorite pastime. Khushi Muhammad went to pains to make her realize but she overlooked her father's advice. Ultimately, being thunderstruck by it, Khushi Muhammad died.

Saiyan used to practice lovemaking with all the comings and goings to amuse herself. One day, there came an income tax officer, Agha Akmal Qazilbash, to her brothel. When Saiyan extended her claws of love, he got entrapped in them. He often used to appear at Saiyan's brothel. They both used to have prolonged conversations that lasted for hours and then they would go into seclusion. Agha proceeded to such a degree in this play of seclusion that he had to marry Saiyan.

After marriage, a daughter was born to Saiyan named Naila. After Naila's birth, Reema was born and then one more baby girl was born to them. When Naila entered adulthood, just like her mother, she started having love affairs. Akmal tried hard to explain to Saiyan so that she should prevent Naila from indulging in such activities. But Saiyan acted evasively and ultimately, Akmal severed his ties with Saiyan and her daughters.

Soon, Saiyan got Naila married but she could not sustain her marriage for long. Hence, she came back home after getting divorced. Their mother made Reema get admitted into a school, but due to her conduct, she was ousted from the school. After some time, Saiyan got Reema deflowered by a noble of Multan and earned a ton of money.

Saiyan's house was adjacent to Anjuman's house on Gul Road. Saiyan often used to say to Nazeeran that one day they would also become well-off. She said that her daughter was no less than anyone else and that she could preside over any man of wealth.

After getting separated from Akmal Qazilbash, Saiyan along with her daughters came to the red-light district in Lahore. On the other hand, Akmal Qazilbash married actress Ismat Tahira. Take note that it was Ismat Tahira's third marriage.

Reema's sister Naila resumed her indecent business after getting divorced. She gathered a considerable amount from this business. From these earnings, she rented an apartment of three rooms in Kareem Park. But a few months later, she left behind her mother and sisters and eloped with a musician.

Reema's Entry into Films

When Reema came to Lahore, she had already hit puberty. Since she had observed her sister, Naila, doing shady business, she was not in need of further guidance. To multiply her earnings, she started dancing as a prostitute. On the other hand, her mother, Saiyan started creating social ties with influential people.

Those days, Chaudhry Ajmal was making a film titled "Qismat," and Iqbal Kashmiri was its director. In this film, a child star (girl) was required. Saiyan told Ajmal Chaudhry that she could fulfill his quest and Chaudhry Ajmal assented to it. Saiyan presented her daughter, who was younger than Reema, in the film. This girl child (Bubbly) played the role of Arfa Siddiqui's childhood.

The song that was filmed by Bubbly is popular to date. Its lyrics go like this:

> *I am my mother's sweetheart*
> *O brother for you I devote myself*
> *But O father, you and I are in dispute*
> *Towards you, I will remain resentful*

In your lap, I am not going to sit
Nor will I ask for dolls & pieces of silk cloth
From you, I will not receive anything
For you listen to me not
Who am I to you?
O father you and I are in dispute

Director Iqbal Kashmiri's film "Qismat" was released on 20 June 1985. "Qismat" did highly profitable business, and it won two awards as well. Many people regard it as Reema's first film while this character, who had a striking resemblance to Reema, was played by her sister, Bubbly.

In a ceremony, Reema was dancing when a well-known director, Javed Fazil's wife, happened to be present at the same ceremony. Reema performed such a mesmerizing dance that everyone kept gazing at her in wonder. At the conclusion of the ceremony, Mrs. Javed Fazil asked Reema for her address.

Now, you must be wondering how, being a resident of a three-room apartment on rent, Reema would progress expeditiously? Its answer lies in the fact that Reema did not use to sit idle at home, rather she had gathered an ample amount from her dances as a prostitute and her tours to the United Arab Emirates. With the help of this amount, she could get transferred from an apartment on rent to a bungalow.

When some time had passed after the aforementioned ceremony, the filmmaker Islam Butt signed Javed Fazil as a director for his film, "Bulandi." Remember that in those days former actress, Neelo, was also visiting Javed Fazil's house often concerning her son, Shan. According to the plot of the film, a teenage couple was needed. Even though Javed Fazil had chosen Shan, finding a heroine was harder. When Javed Fazil talked about it to his wife at his home, then in no time, the thought of Reema surfaced in Mrs. Javed Fazil's mind. When she told Javed Fazil about Reema, he called Reema to assess her. Reema passed the screen test. It was during the shooting of this film that filmmaker Islam Butt got her identity card made. At that time, (in 1989) Reema was 18 years old.

Javed Fazil made great efforts for this film. Reema also danced open-heartedly. "Bulandi" was presented for a screening on 21 September 1990. The film won seven Nigar awards. As the film succeeded, Reema and Shan also became eminent all over Pakistan.

In those days, actress Madiha Shah had also progressed from the TV screen to films. Madiha Shah's first film was "Raja," directed by Iqbal Kashmiri, which was released on 4 July 1990. Her second film was director Altaf Hussain's "Nagina," which was presented to be exhibited on 5 October 1990. The film "Nagina" became highly successful. Owing to that got two new actresses – Reema and Madiha Shah – in 1990. The amusing thing is that Shan acted as a hero in both "Nagina" and "Bulandi." After "Bulandi," filmmakers started rushing toward Reema to cast her. In 1991, Reema worked in "Khatron Ke Khiladi," "Pyar Hi Pyar," "Naag Devta," "Darindagi,"

"Rambo," "Ishq," "Saat Khoon Maaf," "Dil," "Maidan e Jang" and "Sailab."

Reema was an excellent dancer. In every film, Reema's dance was one of the most prominent features. In this respect, Reema was being labeled as a dancer rather than an actress. In many of her statements, Reema clarified that she should not be considered a mere dancer, because she was a fine actress as well. But directors and the general public ignored her.

Reema's Non-Film Scandals

In addition to Reema's film scandals, she had foreign scandals associated with her as well. First, we would throw light on Reema's non-film scandals.

Tours of Arab Countries

It is essential for any actress to visit Arab countries, as going there brings them good fortune. The tours of Babra Shareef, Anjuman, Nadira and Reema held considerable popularity.

When Reema went on United Arab Emirates tours, in a matter of days she gathered a large sum of riyals. After returning from these tours, she left her small house in Kareem Block and got a bungalow constructed in Zeenat Block, Allama Iqbal Town.

During these tours, once she was dancing in an Arab sheikh's festive gathering when he said to Reema that if she removed her upper body clothing, he would give her an additional 200,000. In reply to that Reema said that if she removed all her clothing, would he give her one million? It was owing to such beautiful remarks that made Reema quite renowned in the Arab world.

Sheikh Rasheed and Reema

Who is not aware of Sheikh Rasheed? As we mention his name, Reema's enchanting face appears in our sight.

During his reign, Sheikh Rasheed offered financial aid to Reema with an open heart. The incident of a cheque worth 200,000 must have become engraved on everyone's memory by now. On 13 July 1993, Sheikh Rasheed offered a cheque worth 200,000 to Reema and its number was 82447124.

This cheque had to be cashed through Diyal Singh Branch of UBL bank in Lahore. It was presented to Reema as remuneration for serving the sheikh abundantly on the night of 12 July 1993. But the irony of fate is that six days later the government was abolished and the cheque could not be cashed. In this wise, Reema's exertion on 12 July 1993 went in vain.

This further strengthened Sheikh Rasheed and Reema's relationship. In the days when Sheikh Rasheed held the position of Minister of Culture, in just a matter of twenty days, due to official tasks all his (the one being described here) joints were aching. A wise man suggested to him to plan an excursion to a foreign country, upon which he became prepared forthwith.

On that front, he confirmed a seat for Reema as well for a trip to Switzerland on 21 September 1991. When they were about to leave, the Pakistani newspapers uncovered these goings-on. He canceled the trip immediately. He pleaded with Reema that she need not bother about it as there was no need to go abroad, as they had beauty spots like Murree and Sawat in their own country. He said that they could visit those places to fulfill all they want. Sheikh Rasheed asked Reema's mother many times to allow him to be her son-in-law but she never consented to it. One day, she asked Sheikh Rasheed what the need for marriage was when Reema was always at his service. Further clarifying her point, Reema's mother said that when pure milk was readily available to him, then why bring a buffalo at home? Sheikh Rasheed said that she was right but it was not much fun. After this incident had occurred, Reema's mother asked her to leave no room for insufficiency while serving the sheikh.

Shahbaz Shareef and Reema

In the same manner as Sheikh Rasheed, the former Chief Minister of Punjab was also Reema's admirer. Whenever he used to feel restless, he would call Reema. Reema also used to be at the service of the Chief Minister in a beaming manner.

Shahbaz Shareef's first meeting with Reema was arranged by a filmmaker. Shehbaz Shareef had had many pleasant meetings with Reema. As a price in return for these meetings, he bestowed her with a beautiful bungalow.

During Shahbaz Shareef's reign, Reema had a similar status as it fell to General Rani's lot during General Yahya's reign. By just making a phone call, Reema could gain a plot, permit, or a job.

Reema and Jam Mashooq Ali

Reema and Jam Mashooq's relationship had also come into the limelight. But this relationship emerged abruptly in the form of an accident.

A few years ago, Reema had gone to Karachi concerning shooting of a film. Jam Mashooq Ali's gaze fell upon her. When Reema did not give her consent easily, she was kidnapped. For the whole night along with his friends, he watched her dancing naked, after which he assaulted her. Reema, then, complained about it to Jam Mashooq's father, Jam Sadiq.

When Ghulam Mustafa Khar discovered the aforementioned incident, he gave a statement in the newspaper that he was aware of Jam Mashooq causing mischief in the darkness of night. Jam Mashooq did not respond to this statement, but the next day Reema said in newspapers addressing Mr. Khan that he should hold his tongue and that she was the age of his daughter. After receiving such a reply, Mr. Khan did not retaliate.

Long story cut short, even though Reema got a payment for the assault that night but she had to remain admitted to hospital for three weeks.

Asif Ali Zardari, Nasir Schon and Reema

Asif Ali Zardari was also ardent about girls associated with films. He provided tours to foreign countries for multiple girls but the actress Reema was Asif Ali's beloved source of nourishment. He often used to call Reema in the Marriot Hotel of Islamabad. Neglecting her film engagements, Reema also used to travel to far-off places to please Asif Ali Zardari.

One of Zardari's close friends, Nasir Schon, was also infatuated with Reema. For Nasir Schon, every passing moment was heavy upon him in Reema's absence.

He bought plenty of jewelry for Reema, among which was a diamond necklace worth 1,250,000 rupees. Once, Reema went along with Nasir Schon to Karat Jewelers located in Empire Center. There she demanded another necklace and Nasir Schon presented a prize bond worth 800,000 rupees as an advance payment.

He was a father of four. His wife, Farah, was also an attractive woman but being spellbound by Reema's love, he stopped visiting her house. His wife contacted an elderly man who told him that Reema had cast black magic on Nasir. This made his wife feel worried, and she began abusing and cursing Reema.

Being in Reema's love from head to toe, one day Nasir gave his wife the threat of divorce. He said that he could leave her and their children but that to him, leaving Reema was synonymous with giving up his life.

As a recompense for Nasir Schon's blind love for Reema, she had to visit the hospital twice for abortions. But when there is love, one has to offer such sacrifices.

Reema's Dances Numbers

Alongside working in films, Reema continued her dances as a prostitute as well. A man named Ishaque also made Reema a bungalow in Garden Town. He often used to order Reema to appear for dance numbers but he never defrauded her.

Once, a marriage ceremony of a merchant's son was being held in Gulberg Lahore and there the attendants were throwing 500 and 1000 rupee notes on Reema. After the passage of some time, when a millionaire made an appearance there, he called Reema closer to him. As Reema drew nearer to him, he handed over 100,000 rupees to her, and holding her other hand, he put on a diamond ring on her finger. Feeling blissful, she presented an excellent dance performance the whole night. At the conclusion of the ceremony, the tycoon's friend asked why he had given such a huge amount and a ring to Reema.

Upon this, he said that his arm had grown weary by offering 500 and 1000 Rupee notes again and again.

Reema's New Victim

For the preceding months, Reema had entrapped some new prey. After the film "Nikki Jai Haan," most of Reema's films flopped including "Pasand," "Aik Pagal Si Larki," "Naukar," "Dil To Pagal Hai," "Laung Da Lashkara," "Yaar Chan Warga," and "Pehchan." For this reason, Reema thought of holding the reins of a new victim so that she would face no trouble regarding her expenditures.

Reema's new prey was an industrialist, Sheikh Shehzad. Reema had gained loads of money from him up to now. In addition to that, Shehzad had bought her plenty of jewelry and precious dresses. Reema had now put forth a demand for a Mercedes car. He promised to fulfil her demand but along with that, Shehzad made an offer to Reema to go to America. Reema asked him to fulfill her demand beforehand and then they would go to America.

Reema as a Matchmaker

Just like Musarrat Shaheen, Reema also used to dominate in uniting two hearts. Reema did not wish that two hearts that love each other should depart from this world apart. These days a case of a former hero, Asif Khan's son, was being handled by Reema.

Asif Khan's son, Arbaz Khan, initiated his film career with director Syed Noor's film "Ghoonghat." Arbaz did not work in many films. Nowadays, he is captivated by actress

Khushboo's love. Before making an entrance into films, Khushboo was associated with Sheikh Islam ud Din from Karachi, and for this reason, she also became a mother to a baby girl.

Due to Arbaz and Khushboo's love, Asif Khan became quite mournful. But Reema arranged their meeting in her own house. She made arrangements for their wedding as well. Being influenced by Reema's instigation, Arbaz Khan was not complying with his father.

Khushboo was badly captivated by Arbaz's love. You can affirm this by the fact that a few days ago, Khushboo bought Arbaz Khan a car in installments. Now let's see how far Reema supports them both to the ultimate outcome of this love.

Reema in the Bathroom

This incident happened in the days when director Masood Butt's film, "Sangdill," was being shot in the mesmerizing valleys of Shogran. At this spot, Reema and Moammar Rana's two songs were recorded. On the last day after the conclusion of the shooting and prior to arriving in Lahore, Reema went to the bathroom in her hotel room. It was early in the morning.

Reema unclothed herself and turned on the shower. When cold water falling from the shower came in contact with Reema's body, it led to a strange condition. When Reema stretched herself involuntarily, on the spur of the moment, her sight followed a ventilator above the shower. Reema was frozen for some moments. Reema saw that her sixteen-year-old servant, Aslam (who is a Christian) was standing on a table outside the room and amusing himself with the beautiful sight of Reema's body. Reema put on her clothes and made her way out immediately. She called her special servant, Mastoo, and ordered him to catch Aslam and then she started screaming in a loud voice.

A few minutes later, the whole unit gathered in Reema's room. Mastoo caught Aslam and beat him up. Reema's blood was boiling. To see that body, admirers used to deplete their safety deposit boxes, and Aslam, had dared watch it for free. Reema said that she would hand him over to the police but later on she did not act upon it. Rather she took him with her to Lahore and handed him to Mehmood Butt of Evernew studio, so that his entry to the studio would be banned forever.

Reema's Film Scandals

In addition to non-film scandals, a few of Reema's film scandals became renowned as well. Let's analyze them one by one.

Reema and Shan

Neelo and Riaz Shahid's son Shan began his artistic career with filmmaker Islam Butt's film "Bulandi" at the age of seventeen. Its director was Muhammad Javed Fazil. In "Bulandi," Shan's heroine was Reema, and at the time they both were teenagers. It was during this film that they both started falling for each other. Reema and Shan were going through an emotional phase of their age and at this age, love is usually blind. Sense and intelligence are gone at this age.

In those days, Madiha Shah's film "Nagina" became successful. Shan was the hero in both "Bulandi" and "Nagina." The fun fact is that both Reema and Madiha were showing admiration for Shan. Whenever Reema and Shan had a fight, they did not use to be on speaking terms for many days. As a result, filmmakers had to suffer heavy losses. The actual bone of contention was always Madiha Shah. When Shan used to get closer to Madiha Shah, Reema would become agitated. But as soon as Shan used to focus his attention on Reema and leave out Madiha Shah, then they would reconcile.

Due to this hide and seek, filmmakers had to pay through the nose every now and then. But for Reema and Shan, it was a form of displaying love.

Filmmakers were casting Shan constantly in their films. You can get a sense of this by keeping in view the number of films, which means in the first three years, from "Bulandi" to "Anjuman," Shan worked in 28 films. Along with films, he was enamored by Reema. For this reason, he also took a promise from his mother, Neelo, for getting married to Reema. Shan did not have the slightest idea what the impact of his decision would have on Reema. Reema had made Shan enamored of herself by means of a fake display of love – as she belonged to that market, from where eminent landlords used to leave being bankrupt. But helpless Shan forgot everything, being in love.

Ultimately, one day Reema rejected Shan wretchedly and Babar Ali became the reason for this rejection. Being impressed by his outward prosperity, Reema deserted her companion of early days. On the other hand, Shan had gone too far in love that his return was hard.

After being rejected by Reema, Shan abandoned the Film Industry as well. He became addicted to drugs and grew a grief beard. He isolated himself in a room and lamented over Reema's betrayal.

When Neelo became familiar with this situation, she felt aggrieved. She began explaining to Shan that he was the son of such a father who never made women his weakness. Rather women themselves used to walk around Riaz Shahid. He proved himself by dint of hard work. And that he should get over that streetwalker, as a million girls like her would beg for getting married to him.

This oratory did not put an impact on Shan as he did not want to see any face except that of Reema's. But Neelo Begum did not lose hope, she had faith in her son and that one day he would listen to her. Finally, one day he consented to what his mother said. He decided to start over by working in films. Syed Noor assigned Shan an antagonistic role in the film "Ghoonghat." The film "Ghoonghat" was released on 12 July 1996, and along with the film Shan also became a hit one more time. In this film, Shan won Nigar Award. After this film, Shan had a lively role in director Sangeeta's film "Khilona." Besides that, in Masood Butt's film "Fareb," Shan impressed people with his acting skills.

Now, gradually, Shan started gaining popularity among common people once more. Shan had also forgotten Reema and only his future was lying ahead of him. Despite that, many girls attempted to become a part of Shan's life and among them an actress of Karachi Television, Mishi Khan, was also included. She often used to come from Karachi to Lahore just for the sake of meeting Shan. She made a considerable amount of effort so that she might get married to Shan. When none of Mishi Khan's plans worked, she finally gave up.

Likewise, the Queen of Melody, Noor Jehan's youngest daughter, Neena also loved Shan. She worshipped Shan to the point of obsession. Witnessing her state of madness, Noor Jehan met Neelo and got them engaged. A new actress, Noor, also used to make frequent visits to Shan's house. For the sake of the comfort of her heart, Shan spent a few nights of his life with Noor as well.

In the director Sangeeta's film "Nikah," Shan and Reema had another chance to become united. During the shooting of the film, Reema tried her best to win Shan's attention again but Shan remained indifferent towards Reema. When the film "Nikah" became a super hit, an opportunity came to Reema's hand to draw closer to Shan. But the Shan she was looking for had gone far away from her.

A few of Shan's best films after "Ghoonghat":

Title of Film	Director	Release Date	Outcome
Khilona	Sangeeta	1-November 1996	Successful
Fareb	Masood Butt	10-Oct-1997	Moderate
Nikah	Sangeeta	5-Jun-1998	Successful
King Maker	Pervaiz Rana	31-Jul-1998	Successful
Guns and Roses	Shan	19-Jan-1999	Moderate
Daku Rani	Syed Noor	29-Mar-1999	Successful
Jazba	Hasan Askari	29-Oct-1999	Moderate
Chaudhrani	Hasan Askari	12-Nov-1999	Successful
Ghar Kab Ao Ge	Iqbal Kashmiri	9-Jan-2000	Successful
Yar Badshah	Pervaiz Rana	17-Mar-2000	Successful

Through the aforementioned list of films, you can get an idea of the number of successes that Shan gained in the second period of his career. On the other hand, Reema's graph stooped too low. While she was thinking of her downfall, she discovered that Shan was getting married to a girl, Amna Banday, who did not belong to filmdom. Now, Reema had no choice except to suffer in silence – but what was the use of crying over spilled milk?

Shan's marriage to Mr. Parvez Banday's daughter, Amna, took place on 15 May 2000 on a Monday. Shan's marriage contract was validated by Maulana Ahmed Farooq Madni. The fun fact is that Amna was adored by both Shan and Neelo (Abida Riaz).

Being married to Amna proved auspicious for Shan. After their wedding, the following is a list of Shan's films.

Title of Film	Director	Release Date	
Sulatana Daku	Sangeeta	11-Aug-2000	
Ishtihari Gujjar	Parvez Rana	26-Oct-2000	
Ghulam	Masood Butt	28-Dec-2000	Eid-ul-Fitr
Aag Ka Darya	Iqbal Kashmiri	"	"
Tere Pyar Main	Hasan Askari	"	"
Jag Wala Mela	Parvez Rana	"	"
Dakait	Syed Noor	6-Mar-2001	Eid-ul-Azha
Musalman	Iqbal Kashmiri	"	"
Hukoomat	Masood Butt	"	"
Allah Badshah	Parvez Rana	"	"

On the occasions of Eid-ul-Fitr and Eid-ul-Adha, Shan's eight films were released. The fun fact is that none of Reema's films became a super hit. Apart from that, Shan's film "Khanzada" was released on 25 May 2001. Then, Shan's graph went up. A few days ago, Shan had a successful operation on his piles. Now, he is healthy and working like before in films.

Reema and Babar Ali

Babar Ali started his showbiz career in Karachi Television. He received compliments for showing his excellent acting skills in Qasim Jalali's drama "Labaik." After dramas, Babar Ali headed to films. Director Syed Noor cast Babar in his film "Jeeva" and Shameem Ara cast him in her film "Munda Bigra Jaye." The shooting of "Munda Bigra Jaye" was held in Sri Lanka. In this film, Babar Ali was paired with Reema.

At the time, Reema had an inclination for speaking English and wearing modern dresses. After seeing such a charming and educated man, Reema could not resist. During the film shooting in Sri Lanka, Reema presented herself to Babar Ali. Babar Ali also regarded Reema's desires. After returning from Sri Lanka, Reema was caught up in her regular tasks.

On 3 March 1995, Syed Noor's film "Jeeva" was released, in which Babar Ali's heroine was Resham. This film set new records of success. Babar Ali's pair with Resham became quite a hit. Reema begrudged witnessing Resham's success. Pushing Resham aside, Reema sought refuge in Babar Ali's embrace once again. On 14 April 1995 when "Munda Bigra Jaye" was released, its success became the talk of the town. As Reema was the heroine of this film, that is why she had a stroke of fortune. In those days, the unit of filmmaker Sajjad Gul's film "Jo Dar Gaya Wo Marr Gaya" departed for the Philippines, and Reema and Babar Ali were also included in that unit.

In the Philippines, they enjoyed themselves to their heart's content. For the whole day, they used to strike love notes while in the evening having fun in bed.

A few days later, as the unit of Shameem Ara's film "Miss Istanbul" went abroad, they both got the full benefit out of this seclusion. There, Reema followed Babar Ali like his shadow. She was enamored by Babar to such an extent, that she, herself, would wash his filthy clothes. She had completely held Babar's reins in her hands. They say that Reema is a witch and it was hard for Babar to free himself from her ruling.

On returning to Pakistan, Reema got the news published in newspapers that they were getting married. In Karachi, Babar Ali's family took offense over it because they were quite religious, and accepting a daughter of a prostitute as their daughter-in-law was highly discreditable for them. On the other hand, Reema's mother, Saiyan was also melancholic as she did not want to let this golden bird get separated from her under any circumstances. Reema and Babar Ali worked in 29 films together among which "Love 95," "Chour Machaye Shor," "Mamla Garbar Hai," "Sarak," "Najaiz," "Aulad Ki Qasam," "Dunya Hai Dill Walon Ki," "Khuda Jane," "Raja Pakistani" and "Devar Deewane" are included.

Their relationship had just matured when Babar's films started to become flops. Reema began overlooking Babar Ali on many occasions. Babar Ali, being helpless, was reduced to silence. As he was also a human, hence he had an understanding of what was about to happen to him. He had become certain about the fact that Reema had entrapped a new victim and that is why she wants to part with him. Babar Ali consoled himself and pulled away from her.

Nowadays, Babar Ali has appeared as a villain in films. In "Ghar Kab Ao Ge," "Aag Ka Darya," "Nooran" and "Dakait," Babar's Ali character was quite appreciated.

How did Reema's Downfall Occur?

Reema had started making money as soon as she passed the threshold of adulthood. Through her amorous gestures, she had made several landlords and nobles go bankrupt. Nasir Schon's wife had given a curse to Reema from the bottom of her heart. And when Reema betrayed Shan, then his mother, Neelo had also cursed her. Besides that, when Reema had thrown Babar Ali away as one does after sucking a ripened mango, he uncovered the bruises he developed from Reema's betrayal while prostrating in front of Allah.

With regards to having a number-one priority, Reema fought with many contemporary heroines among whom Madiha Shah, Resham, Meera and Saima are included.

When Meera won the hearts of the public by displaying a fine performance in "Khilona" and "Chief Sahib," then Reema demeaned herself by having fisticuffs with Meera. Likewise, being dismayed by Resham's popularity, she opened a front against her.

Reema's behavior with director Iqbal Kashmiri and Masood Butt was also transgressing. When Reema was working on Iqbal Kashmiri's film "Pyar Hi Pyar Main," she fought concerning the dates of shooting and ruined many of Iqbal Kashmiri's days.

In the same wise, she dishonored Masood Butt in the film "Billo 420." It was Reema's yearning that Abrar ul Haq's song

"Aaja Ni Beh Ja Cycle Te" be picturized on her. Filmmakers Jamshed Zafar and Masood Butt did not approve of it. They wanted to shoot this song with Saima but ultimately, being annoyed, Masood Butt filmed this with Saima, Reema, and Nargis collectively.

In recent months, Reema was working on Masood Butt's film "Hukoomat." Just one dance number had been filmed yet, and Reema left the film while it was incomplete. It led to a heavy loss for Masood Butt. Later on, Masood Butt cast Sana in that film.

The Divine Power was witnessing the aforementioned spectacle of Reema but it was letting go of her. At last, one day Reema committed such a deed that The Divine Power pushed her into darkness and all of her films began to flop.

In the annual program of ZeeTv Indian Antakshari, Sajjad Ali, Atiqa Odho and Reema participated from Pakistan. On this program, Sajjad Ali, Atiqa Odho and Reema sang the lyrics of "Dill Dill Pakistan" and "Jaan Jaan Hindustan." This program had not come on the air yet, and a wave of outrage emerged against the abovementioned artists all over Pakistan. People ignored Sajjad Ali and Atiqa Odho but as far as Reema was concerned, people had quite provocative emotions toward her. Reema was declared a non-believer and traitor. Even many religious scholars also declared her worthy of killing. After returning to Pakistan, Reema resorted to the media to prove her innocence. A discussion was recorded on PTV in Reema's favor. In addition to that, when she was invited to Tariq Aziz's show, people sitting in the hall booed her. Reema fled from the show. After this incident occurred, people abandoned watching Reema's released films in the cinema. On 31 December 1999, when this program was displayed on ZeeTV then the words "Jaan Hindustan" were omitted from the program. It was done just for the sake of the Pakistani public developing a good opinion about Reema but it was too late.

The mills of God grind slowly, but they grind very fine. Reema was entangled in a vortex due to her own wiles. Every film used to flop in which Reema appeared. Let us enlighten you about the details of those films.

Film Title	Director	Release Date	Outcome
Aik Pagal Si Larki	Altaf Hussain	27-Aug-1999	Flopped
Naukar	Hasnain	15-Oct-1999	Flopped
Qismat	Sangeeta	22-Oct-1999	Flopped
Dil To Pagal Hai	Sangeeta	29-Oct-1999	Flopped
Laung Da Lashkara	Altaf Hussain	18-Feb-2000	Flopped
Yar Chan Warga	Shahid Rana	18-Feb-2000	Flopped
Pehchan	Masood Butt	17-Mar-2000	Flopped
Mujhe Chaand Chahiay	Shan	17-Mar-2000	Flopped
Pasand	Altaf Hussain	21-Apr-2000	Flopped
Sangdill	Masood Butt	5-May-2000	Flopped
Khuda Ke Chour	Parvez Rana	19-May-2000	Flopped
Banarsi Chour	Masood Butt	23-Jun-2000	Flopped
Billo 420	Masood Butt	29-Sep-2000	Successful
Barood	Suhail Khan	20-Oct-2000	Flopped
Mukhra Chan Warga	Masood Butt	20-Apr-2001	Flopped

Reema and Saud

Reema, who had left Shan and Babar Ali, and had also held Moammar Rana encaptivated by the shadow of her beautiful tresses for some days, was now waiting for a new hero's arrival. It was then that Saud and Reema came across each other.

Reema had never let anyone become her necessity to date. But with regard to Saud, she seemed powerless. Take note that it was the same Saud whom Reema had wished to cut from Syed Noor's film, "Hawayein," to cast Babar Ali in it. But all her efforts had gone in vain.

In Karachi, at the conclusion of the film shooting of "Barood," Reema called Saud to Lahore over a phone call. Then for four consecutive days, they kept shooting for their love in a hotel in Karachi. Due to their love affair, the shooting of Masood Butt's film "Mukhra Chan Warga" had to be called off twice.

In September 2000, Reema came along with Saud to Multan while wearing a veil. When they were having a meal at a restaurant, people recognized them. After staying in Multan for two days, they left for Lahore. Reema considers herself a witty lady. She has made a fool of many people. But in the case of Saud, it was her who was made a fool of. Saud promised Reema to make her settle in America, which was why Reema pursued Saud.

A few months ago, on 20 December 2000, Reema left director Masood Butt's film "Hukoomat" incomplete and departed for

America along with Saud. She performed in many musical shows there and all the earnings fell into Saud's hands. She used to live in Saud's flat. For the sake of living there, she had proved herself as Saud's wife in the documents. After acting for this fake drama of being a husband and wife, they both returned from America to Lahore on 22 February 2001.

In film circles, it became renowned that Reema and Saud had got married but both of them refuted it. Let's see, when the public becomes aware of their reality.

Saima

MULTAN'S GIFT NO. 3
SAIMA

From Multan to Syed Noor

A height of five feet and six and a half inches; long, black, and thick hair; a glowing and radiant complexion; wide, intoxicating eyes; a sharp nose; juicy lips and a sexy body – the name of the owner of all these is Saima.

Saima's domestic name was Sumera. Her terms of affection at home are Ghuncha, Khhachi, Khakwani and sometimes she likes to be called Syed Zadi. To date, only her mother calls her this.

As soon as she passed the threshold of adulthood, the citizens of Multan began drinking the nectar of this flower by squeezing it. This ripened fruit used to fall in anyone's lot for an exchange of even a small amount. Whoever drank this delicious drink had to bring his friends on the next visit to get entertained at Saima's doorstep. This flowing river quenched the thirst of many Multanis. And these events kept occurring for many years. Saima used to drive rashly on the roads of Multan.

When people used to introduce her, they would compulsively highlight the fact that she was the one who violated traffic light rules. Multanis would not have thought that this flowing river would be directed to Lahore.

One day, Saima's mother went to Lahore along with her. Saima's married sister, who was three years older than her, was already residing in Lahore. After coming to Lahore, Saima resided in the royal area for some time. At that time, Saima was more than 25 years old. Then, she got from Ali Sufyan Afaqi, a well-known journalist, a bungalow on rent which had the address 20B Model Town, Lahore. Saima's mother had introduced them as an escaped family to Mr. Afaqi. Little did he know what disturbance they would cause later on. Saima was a veteran lady of Multan; she had complete faith in her amorous gestures. And that she could make Lahori people come after her whenever she desired to.

In Lahore, Nagina Khanum's warehouse was highly prominent for exhibitionism. Therefore, Saima also took refuge in that warehouse. Nagina Khanum used to empty the pockets of people belonging to every school of thought, among whom politicians, landlords, government officers and industrialists are eminent. Nagina Khanum had colorful butterflies of all ages who used to be available to serve for twenty-four hours. Just by making a single phone call, she could make happen the greatest of tasks.

As Saima was quite alluring, that is why customers were more enamored of her.Seeing this, Saima's mother used to feel delighted that her child had good fortune. Seeing her, she used to feel joyous. Director Akhtar Khan used to visit different warehouses in search of enchanting butterflies. One day, when he arrived at Nagina Khanum's warehouse,he couldn't go back. In Saima, he witnessed that feminine attraction that he had never seen before in anyone. In a matter of few days, Akram Khan became a captive of Saima's tresses and worldly matters slipped out of his mind. He used to remain asleep by keeping his head in Saima's lap for hours and the warmth of Saima's body used to provide him with coolness. One day, being in a similar state, he offered her work on his film "Khatarnak." Saima accepted this offer.

Take note that he is the same Akram Khan who made the film "Khan Zada" and introduced the new actress Najma in it. And he had filmed a sexy song on her while she was semi-clothed, and the lyrics of the song go like this:

> *Amorous glances when meet, keep exchanging them, say not a word if you wish to get amused by love then keep swelling your heart with comfort, say not a word*

When the film was released on 11 April 1975, Owing to this song and Najma's naked dance, people all over Pakistan rushed to cinemas. The film was a super hit. Using this very song, Akram Khan also made a film named "Khan Zada" 26 years later. In that film, Saima and Shan played central roles. When this film was released on 25 May 2001, the film admirers were quite disappointed. The film flopped as soon as it was released.

In. "Khatarnak," Saima was Sultan Rahi's heroine. It was Saima's first-ever shot with Sultan Rahi. When Saima delivered her dialogues on set, everyone was awe-struck because Saima got her shots completed with high self-confidence. After some time, Sultan Rahi whispered in Akram Khan's ears that Saima was really dangerous.

The film "Khatarnak" was released on 19 October 1990 but it was unsuccessful. Even though the film became unsuccessful, in the form of Saima, the film industry had found a heroine for Punjabi films.

Kaifi and Saima

Actor and director Kaifi was a brother of famous singer Inayat Hussain Bhatti, and was the paternal uncle of TV actor Abbas. Kaifi had started acting at a young age. Apart from that, he directed "Jind Jaan," "Challenge," "Zulm Da Badla," "Ultimatum," "Sacha Sauda," "Sajjan Dushman," "Mile Ga Zulm Da Badla," "Haq Sach," "Bilawal," "Muhammad Khan," "Macch Jail," "Taqat" and "Sajjan Payara."

Kaifi and Inayat Hussain Bhatti (Bhatti Brother) were famous for the fact that they used to offer chances to new girls in films, after keeping them as their mistresses for a long period.

For instance, both brothers used to have fun with a famous actress, Rani, in bed for a long period and then gave her a chance in "Sajjan Payara," "Jind Jaan" and "Sacha Sauda." In the same way they also treated Ghazala and Khanum. When Sindhi film heroine Chakori came to Lahore with Mushtaq Changezi, Mr. Kaifi became her admirer. After a few beautiful meetings, he married her. And when he (the respected one) was bored of her, he left her along with children.

Chakori had played the role of Daro Nattni in the renowned film "Maula Jutt." From 1996–97, she won the hearts of admirers by playing the role of a Khanum prostitute in the drama "Janam Ki Maili Chadar" in Tamaseel Theatre, Lahore.

Saima had not become free from Akram Khan's clutches yet when Kaifi started making efforts to win Saima's heart. He was thinking of making Saima the queen of his heart. You can have an idea of Kaifi's mental state by the fact that he sold his bungalow for 2.5 million rupees, and started a new film, "Marshal Law," for Saima. To make Saima appear enchanting, Kaifi made a set worth 300,000 rupees, installed in Shah Noor Studio. This set was so magnificent that people from remote places used to visit Shah Noor Studio to get a view of it. Kaifi left no stone unturned to highlight Saima. He used to spend his whole day in Saima's bungalow. He did not use to leave her room for hours; he even wrote the script for the film in her room.

A time came when Kaifi used to appear on every set on which she would be working. When a friend inquired, Kaifi said that he could see the second Chakori in Saima's face.

He said that Saima was like a beautiful gift that had descended from the sky for him and he did not want to get it wasted. On the other hand, Saima also showed Kaifi a new path of licentiousness by opening her heart and by leaving herself at his mercy.

While this love connection was going on, Saima became pregnant. Upon this, Kaifi and Saima's families became quite troubled. In those days, Saima was immersed in films. Kaifi took Saima to London so that they could get rid of the torment of pregnancy. After Saima went abroad, her family publicized the news that Saima was possessed by supernatural beings and for that sake, she had been exiled from that area.

As soon as Saima come out of the influence of their possession, she would return. A month later, Saima returned from London and those supernatural beings were gone in reality. After coming back from London, Saima started appearing even more alluring. After Kaifi, when many other lovers began repeating the same patterns of possession by supernatural beings, she left Kaifi and went far away from him. Kaifi was disheartened by this incident. He would not have thought that a daughter of a prostitute craved wealth, over a companion.

Seth Javed and Saima

When a prostitute falls in love, she offers her everything as a sacrifice for her beloved. Whomever a prostitute loved, he used to have a stroke of fortune. Many years ago, when a prostitute from the red-light district fell in love with actor Shahid, she transformed his whole life. Seema helped Shahid financially and physically. Even then, the credit for introducing Shahid to films also went to Seema. Take note that it is the same Seema who had played the role of Rani, as the wife of Sultan Rahi's brother in the film "Maula Jutt."

In the same way, actress Saima loved an industrialist, named Javed from Sialkot. She worshipped Javed by breaking the boundaries of society. Whenever she used to get captured in Javed's embrace, she would loosen herself to such an extent that it was as if her body was lifeless.Saima would find such pleasure while being secluded with Javed, which was many times more than the millions in wealth given by any noble. Saima was also very happy in the sense that she herself loved someone. But her happiness did not last long as after some time, Javed left her and went far away.

That moment was very disastrous for Saima. She had not even loved Javed with all her heart and her boat of love had already sunk. She became very sad and started drinking heavily. She was often found drunk in Suman Abad (Lahore).

Apart from Javed, Saima had also established love relations with businessmen like Azeem Gilani from Multan and Kamal Khan from Lahore. But both of the relations were business types and she looted both of them a lot.

Sultan Rahi and Saima

Sultan Rahi was a double-faced man. On the one hand, he used to build mosques, perform Hajj and help orphans while on the other hand, he extended his hand of friendship to filmic girls. You have read the details of such relationships in the story of Anjuman. Sultan Rahi had developed a soft spot in his heart for Saima from the very first day. He often recommended that filmmakers should cast Saima. Anjuman also felt this thing and once she said to Sultan Rahi, "Mr. Rahi, do also recommend us too." He listened to Anjuman and remained silent.

After Asia and Anjuman, Saima has done more films with Sultan Rahi

Name of Film	Director	Release Date
Khatarnaak	Akram Khan	19-Oct-1990
Qadil Qaidi	Khalifa	13-Sep-1991
Kharaak	Safdar Hussain	12-Jun-1992
Parinday	Altaf Qamar	9-Oct-1992
Babbra	Zahoor Hussain Gilani	27-Nov-1992
Sher Ali	Masood Butt	25-Dec-1992
Irada	Hassan Askari	1-Jan-1993
Khuda Gawah	Masood Butt	25-Mar-1993
Ghunda	Shahid Rana	27-Aug-1993
Purana Paapi	Akram Khan	3-Sep-1993
Aan	Hassan Askari	24-Dec-1993
Zameen Asmaan	Hasnain	22-May-1994
Traffic Jam	Khalifa Syed Ahmed	23-Dec-1994
Vehshi Aurat	Ali Raza	3-Mar-1995

Chaudhry Badshah	Altaf Hussain	27-Oct-1995
Jungle ka Qanoon	Masood Butt	1-Dec-1995
Sakhi Badshah	Masood Butt	21-Feb-1996
Rani Khan	Azmat Nawaz	13-Dec-1996
Kala Raj	Faiz Malik	18-Apr-1997
Sukhan	Din	5-Dec-1997

Javed Sheikh and Saima

Javed Sheikh has a long line of girls coming into his life. After actor Shahid, he had the most scandals in the film world. He kept a relationship with Neeli for many years. They often quarreled with each other apart from love. Whenever Javed got angry with Neeli, he would immediately turn to other girls because he could not spend even a single day without a girl.

The quarrel between them would go on for a few days and then they would reconcile. As soon as Javed reconciled with Neeli, he would avoid the new girl. The lives of many girls were ruined due to their quarrels, but Javed Sheikh never noticed this.

After Sultan Rahi, Javed Sheikh was of great importance for Saima, but in those days he was in love with Neeli. The following are a few films with Saima as the heroine opposite Javed Sheikh.

Name of Film	Director	Release Date
Dill Lagi	Zahoor Hussain Gilani	13-Jan-1992
Hussain Ki Baraat	Iqbal Kashmiri	5-Apr-1992
Mohabbbat ke Saudagar	Jaan Muhammad	5-Apr-1992

Khoon ka Qarz	M.A Rasheed	28-Aug-1992
Ilaqa Ghair	Mumtaz Ali Khan	17-Sep-1993
Dill Wale	Akram Khan	31-Oct-1997

Some time ago, when Javed Sheikh's relationship with Neeli became strained, he turned to Saima. He told his friends, "Neeli has no value. I have found a very beautiful girl; I will do her photo session and let you know." When he did a photo session of Saima and showed it to his friends, they were really stunned. Saima looked very unique in that session. On that occasion, Javed Sheikh announced that Saima would be the heroine of his film "Chief Sahib". When Neeli came to know about it, she abused Javed Sheikh and said, "Javed Sheikh uses my money and will make the film Chief Sahib with my money."

It should be remembered that Neeli had taken ten million rupees from Sarfaraz Merchant for the film "Chief Sahib." When Javed Sheikh was travelling to Istanbul for the purpose of shooting with Saima, some friends made him reconcile with Neeli. Javed Sheikh left Saima and took Neeli with him to Istanbul and poor Saima remained empty handed.

After the film release, Neeli and Javed Sheikh had a fight again. In 1999, when Mian Farzand Ali signed Javed Sheikh as the director for his film "Mujhe Jeene Dou," he contacted Saima again. Saima accepted the role and also did some shooting for the film. On the other side, Neeli reconciled with Javed Sheikh again and he cast Neeli after removing Saima from the film.

When Javed Sheikh asked Neeli to do some shooting abroad, she refused on the spot. When Javed Sheikh contacted Saima, she refused him and told him not to try to meet her in future. In those days, Saima had gone far into a relationship with Syed Noor and now the way back was looking very difficult. She did very well by rejecting Javed Shaikh as the film "Muhje Jeene Dou" was rejected by the fans when it was released on 3rd September 1999. In this way she saved her film future.

Syed Noor and Saima

Syed Noor has a higher place among the directors of the present era. Nowadays his name is considered a guarantee of success for a film. Syed Noor and Saima have now become one name. Like in previous eras, Muhammad Ali and Zeba, Javed Sheikh and Neeli, Reema and Shaan, Shaan and Babra Sharif etc. were inseparable from each other.

How was Syed Noor and Saima's relationship established? Before commenting on the current status of relationship between the two, we will go into Syed Noor's past.

Syed Noor's family is among the patrons of the shrine of Shah Abu Al-Aali – may Allah send blessings upon him (Gawalmandi, Lahore). His family used to live off the donations collected at the shrine. By profession, his father was a booking clerk in a local cinema. His film career began as an assistant director to S. Sulaiman. He spent a few years as his disciple and learned a lot. After that, he was also assistant to the director Iftikhar Malik.

Shamsi Sheikh

In those days, Syed Noor fell in love with a new actress named Shamsi Sheikh, who was given a chance by Shamim Aara in her film "Playboy" and later she also got married to Syed Noor through Shamim Aara. The marriage lasted only for eighteen days and Syed Noor divorced her on the nineteenth day. Syed Noor was very fond of writing stories. His first film as a screenwriter was "Society Girl."

"Society Girl" was Sangeeta's directorial debut. When it was released on April 16, 1976, the film fans declared it a success. After this success, Syed Noor's motivation increased and he wrote "Sohra Te Jawai, Muft Barr, Wardi, Mr. Aflatun, Miss Singapore, Dehleez, Zid, Qasam and Halchal." From the beginning, Syed Noor was accused of copying films. Film critics often wrote that his films were based on plagiarism, but he did not care about such things.

After Shamsi Sheikh, Syed Noor fell in love with famous dancer Parveen Bobby. She also loved Syed Noor and even used to buy Syed Noor clothes in return for his love. She became the mother of a girl child in this love game and Syed Noor left her.

Similarly, another girl came into Syed Noor's life who used to act as a comedian on stage and TV. The name of this comic actress was Romana, who was once the lover of actor Ali Ijaz. After Ali Ijaz, she befriended Syed Noor. At that time, Romana was very famous and nobody recognized Syed Noor. Syed

Noor had promised a lot for their marriage. She started arranging her dowry and when her dowry was completed, Syed Noor broke up with her. After that incident, Romana has not recovered till date.

Syed Noor also worked as an actor in two films, one of which was "Mr. Aflatun," directed by Naseem Haider. It was written by Syed Noor himself. The second film was director Younis Rathore's "Judai." Both the films flopped badly.

Apart from this, Syed Noor also hosted a film song program on PTV. After Romana, he became interested in Rukhsana, who was a journalist. Both of them came closer to each other and got married finally. Despite life's small quarrels, this marriage has remained strong to date.

While writing the stories of the films, one day Syed Noor got the idea that he should also direct the films. Thus, as a director, he made his first film, "Qasam," which featured Saleem Sheikh, Iram Hassan, Nadeem and Rustam. It was released on 24 December 1993 and became a hit due to the good directing of Syed Noor. It also won several awards.

On 3 March 1995, Syed Noor's second film "Jeeva" was released, in which the couple of Babar Ali and Resham became a hit. On September 1, 1995, the third film "Sargam" was released. The fourth film "Chur Machaye Shor" was released on 22 March 1996. The fifth "Hawain" was released in May 1996. All the first five films of Syed Noor were super hits and thus he was biginning to be considered among the best directors of the film industry.

How Did Syed Noor and Saima Become Friends?

After Sultan Rahi's death, the production of Punjabi films had almost stopped. Since Saima was often the heroine of Sultan Rahi, she also became idle. Her condition worsened and she felt as if someone in her family had died. One day a well-wisher seeing her condition said to her, "Do not lose heart, today Syed Noor's star is on the rise; build a relationship with him and all your problems will be solved." Saima liked the idea and made a program to develop relations with Syed Noor. One day, she went to Syed Noor to shower her beauty on him. Syed Noor fell in love with Saima after she showed her prostitute-like coquetries to him.

When Syed Noor asked Saima the reason for her coquetries, he found out that she wanted to act in Syed Noor's film. Thus, Syed Noor gave Saima the role of a prostitute in his film "Ghunghat." When the film was released on July 12, 1999, both the film and Saima became successful. With the success of the film, Saima and Syed Noor became very close which was a danger alarm for Rukhsana Noor. Everyone started telling Rukhsana Noor the stories of Saima and Syed Noor's love affair. She had full faith in her husband. But still a thin line of doubt began to haunt her.

In March 1997, when Syed Noor arrived in Singapore with the unit of the film "Deewarein," Rukhsana also accompanied

Syed Noor in that tour. Saima had a unique role in that film. During the shooting, Rukhsana would suddenly approach Saima and Syed Noor. Both were very worried about the situation. However, Rukhsana also did not lose heart, yet she was unable to catch both of them red-handed. She returned to Pakistan having regret in her heart.

Saima and Syed Noor started the drama of secretly meeting in Pakistan. You can imagine Saima's madness from the fact that some time ago when the director Kaifi was shooting for the film "Jeena Yahan, Marna Yahan" in the beautiful valleys of Kalar Kahar, Saima pretended to change her clothes for the second shot of the shoot. When she did not return after a long time, Kaifi became worried. He sent a man to Saima's room and found that she was missing along with her car. He could not tolerate Saima's behavior and canceled the shoot. Meanwhile, Saima drove her car and came to Syed Noor in Lahore. She said to Syed Noor that she was missing him in the beautiful valleys of Kalar Kahar, so she did not consider it appropriate to stay there.

Kaifi returned to Lahore and complained about Saima to MAAP Chairman Yusuf Khan. Similarly, once Syed Noor was shooting for the film "Zewar" in Reema's bungalow while Saima was shooting for Masood Butt's film "Jise De Maula" in the studio. Saima intentionally wore a loose dress for the shoot. When she went in front of Masood Butt wearing that dress, he scolded Saima and canceled the shoot in anger, seeing her ill-fitting dress. Saima quickly reached Reema's house to meet

Syed Noor, but by that time he had left there. When Reema saw Saima coming towards her, she immediately asked, "Hi Mrs. Noor, who are you looking for?" Hearing this, Saima just smiled and went back to look for Syed Noor.

From the above-mentioned incidents, you must have understood how much love there is between Saima and Syed Noor. After entering Syed Noor's life, Saima acted in some of his films.

Name of Film	Release Date	Outcome
Ghunghat	12-Jul-1996	Successful
Muhafiz	30-Jan-1998	Flop
Deewarein	22-May-1998	Successful
Doupatta Jal Raha Hai	28-Aug-1998	Successful
Churiyan	16-Oct-1998	Super hit & Record Winner
Daku Rani	29-Mar-1999	Successful
Angare	9-Jan-2000	Flop
Jungle Queen	17-Mar-2000	Flop
Billi	21-Jul-2022	Flop
Mehndi Wale Hath	25-Aug-2000	Successful
Baiti	13-Oct-2000	Flop
Dill Kach Da Khadona	2-Feb-2001	Success
Daket	6-Mar-2001	Medium

Out of the above 14 films, 7 failed and thus the success ratio stood at 50%. Apart from Syed Noor, Saima has also acted in films with other actors whose details are as follows.

Name of Film	Director	Release Date	Outcome
Pardesi	Parvez Rana	27-Feb-1998	Successful
Kingmaker	Parvez Rana	31-Jul-1998	Medium
Dou Boond Pani	Sangeeta	30-Oct-1998	Flop
Koila	Masood Butt	19-Jan-1999	Medium
Dekha Jai Ga	Nasir Adeeb	30-Apr-1999	Flop
Jazba	Hasan Askari	29-Oct-1999	Medium
Ghar Kab Aao Ge	Iqbal Kashmiri	9-Jan-2000	Successful
Yaar Badshah	Parvez Rana	17-Mar-2000	Successful
Sultana Daku	Sangeeta	11-Aug-2000	Successful
Aag Ka Darya	Iqbal Kashmiri	28-Dec-2000	Successful
Hakumat	Masood Butt	6-Mar-2001	Medium
Khanzada	Akram Khan	25-May-2001	Medium

All the above films starred Shaan as the hero along with Saima.

Marriage of Saima and Syed Noor

Ever since Syed Noor and Saima became friends, people have been making strange comments about them. For example:

1. The relationship between Syed Noor and Saima is like that of Javed Sheikh and Neeli.
2. Since Syed Noor's family is in the list of progenitor Abu Al-Muali's successors and these people also write talismans, therefore he kept Saima under his control through a talisman so that she could not leave him.
3. Some people believe that the two had a business relationship.

4. Close friends also revealed that they had got married in Rawalpindi.

Mr. Bukhari's Prediction

The lineage of Mr. S.S. Bukhari reaches to Pir Makki. He often makes his predictions about the film industry. A few days ago, he said that Syed Noor and Saima will separate in 2001, otherwise their future will be dark. Earlier, Mr. Bukhari had predicted the flops of Syed Noor's five films, which came true. Among the flops are "Lakhoun mein Aik," "Baiti," "Jungle Queen," "Angare" and "Billi." The fifth film flopped in 2000.

Now let's see how true Mr. Bukhari's prediction regarding the separation of the two proves to be.

1. A few days ago, despite forbidden by Syed Noor, Saima agreed to work in director Shaan's film "Musa."
2. Similarly, Saima has befriended an industrialist and is taking millions of rupees from him. When this came to Syed Noor's notice, he forbade Saima, to which she replied, "Films do not meet my expenses. If you can bear my expenses, I will turn away from the industry."

Considering the abovementioned, it looks like Mr. Bukhari's prediction is going to be correct.